Tali
xoxo
Theresa

THIRST

Incubus Tamed
Book 1
By
Theresa Hissong

Cover Design:
Custom eBook Covers

Editing by:
Heidi Ryan
Amour the Line Editing

Cover Model:
Cody Criswell

Cover Photographer:
Randy Sewell w/
RLS Model Images

Other Books by Theresa Hissong:

Dedication:

Cody Criswell...This one's for you.

Contents:

Chapter 1
Cassius

I hate myself.

The thought blows through my mind as I drink from my victim's vein. The thick, coppery taste of a woman's blood is my weakness; her body is the temple I must worship. It is within the depths of her body where I find life, and with life, I find my disgust of living.

"*Cassius*," she moans as the loss of blood causes her to weaken.

I will not kill her. No, she will live, but after I am done with her, she will not be the same. When she is found, my marks and seed will be absent from her body. This female will not remember the past few days. She will wake up confused after I put her into a comatose state before feeding from her vein. If she is a previous victim of mine, she will start to have episodes of insanity. After several sexual encounters with the same incubus, she will die.

There was a time, almost three hundred years ago, when I was out of control. I've killed women for their blood. I've had sex with them on multiple occasions, taking their souls in the process. I'd leave them in dark alleyways, behind abandoned buildings, in seedy motel rooms, or in their expensive mansions with no care in the world. In the beginning of my new life, I craved it all.

I still do.

Only now, I am older, stronger you could say, and I've learned how to get the things I need to survive without taking a human life. I've found others like myself, but without them, I am a monster…the demon from your nightmares.

The presence of another immortal jerks me from my thoughts. The need to protect my food rushes through my body. My hand covers the female's mouth as I bare my bloody fangs at the shadow crouching in the windowsill. She squirms beneath me, but my instinct to fight outweighs my need to fuck.

"Cassius, you need come now," a voice says. It is a voice I know. "We must go."

"Leave me, Salvatore," I growl, bearing my fangs. I push harder on the woman's mouth as she begins to scream. I haven't taken enough for her to pass out and lose her memories, yet. Her body tightens, so I thrust once more to keep her pussy primed even though Salvatore watches us from the window.

"Finish," he barks. "Knock her out. If you are not outside in five minutes, I will come back, and I'm in no mood to fight with you tonight. We have bigger problems."

"Fuck," I snarl, knowing if he has come to interrupt my feeding, something has happened in our territory.

"I don't know why you don't sedate them right away," he states and gives me a stern look.

I'd never admit it to him, but I like them to fight me a little. The sex, it's mundane to me. The demon inside me likes them coherent for as long as possible before I have to take their souls. Sedating them during most of the act eats away at what's left of my own human soul.

"Leave me," I repeat.

He falls backwards off the ledge, leaving me alone to finish what I came here to do. The slide of my cock quiets the whore beneath me. She orgasms when I sink my fangs into her vein again. My body coils as I feel the life force of the prostitute bleeding into my body. My energy awakens as hers slowly fades. When I release her vein and remove my hand from her mouth, she moans again as my cock swells inside her body. My release is intense, but I do not shout with desire. There is no pleasure in what I am doing. There hasn't been for a while now.

"I'm sorry," I whisper as her body goes lax and she closes her eyes, never to remember what has transpired over the last few hours.

My pants are no further down than below my cock when I back away from her body. I scoop up my shirt, shaking off the dust and whatever else coats the floor of this apartment.

The night is cool as I escape out the window, clinging to the side of the building to close the window. I leave no fingerprints, therefore, there will be no evidence of my arrival or departure.

"What the fuck is going on?" I snap at Salvatore when I find him smoking a cigarette in the alleyway behind the building. He has lipstick marks on the side of his neck, telling me he recently came from feeding off one of the females he met at our last location.

"There's a succubus in our midst," he rattles off, gritting his teeth.

"Did she request approval to be here?" Victor, Salvatore, and myself are the only incubi in the area. Therefore, this is our territory. There are hundreds of cities in the world, and we've spread out to keep our victims to a minimum. Too many soul suckers in one area can cause questions to arise. The humans will get nosey, and we could be exposed.

"She did not," he says, leaning against the wall.

"Who told you she was here?" I press.

"The gargoyles," he replies. Gargoyles are our eyes and ears in the territory. They are servants by nature, wanting to please their leaders. Memphis and Xavier belong to us, and they know their place in our coven. "They encountered her about an hour ago in a bar on the east side of town."

"Where is she now?" I ask, feeling anger boil inside me. As much as I hate this life, I don't want to die. Dying is not an option for me, because the alternative is *Hades*. The real one.

"They lost her," he informs me, blowing out a cloud of smoke as he curses under his breath. "One of them said she scoped out the place, had a few drinks, and pushed away several of the males who approached her. Now, why would a beautiful succubus be in a bar full of men just to have some drinks and leave without coming to me for approval?"

"I'll find Victor and we will hunt for her tonight," I offer. As much as I hate being what I am, I know that being exposed to the humans would be so much worse.

"Find her and bring her to me," he orders, then vanishes into the night.

I lean against the brick exterior of the building and pull out my phone. A quick text to Victor gets me the address of where we will meet. I visualize the bar in my mind and close my eyes. When I open them, I am in a dark corner of the parking lot.

A few drunk humans stumble out into the night. I don't care if they're driving home or not. At this point, I just want to find this succubus and be on my way. Having someone on our turf that doesn't belong puts everyone in danger.

It's no surprise I find the two gargoyles in the bar, taking shots as they enjoy what was supposed to be their night off. They are always available and at my side when I need them, and even when we force them to relax, they're always on guard.

"Xavier...Memphis," I greet as I lean against

the bar top at Xavier's side. He stiffens, but slowly turns in his seat. Both of them have steel-gray eyes that pierce right through you. In fact, they all do. It's one of the ways to identify them from humans. "Where's Victor?"

"He's coming," Memphis confirms, tossing back his drink.

The bartender stops by and asks for my order. I pay him for two shots of tequila to calm my energy, then turn back to the gargoyles. They're nervous, and I can't blame them. If we don't have control over who comes into this town, things will get ugly.

Again…*Hades*.

Yeah, no one wants to go there.

Victor arrives by the time the bartender brings us another round. Memphis and Xavier take their drinks and move away from the bar. We find a secluded booth by the emergency exit and take our seats.

"What happened?" I ask, taking my shot.

"We sensed her when she came in," Memphis says, his eyes darkening. "She's a succubus alright. Long, blonde hair, big tits, and a helluva ass on that one. Whoever changed her was a lucky son-of-a-bitch."

"Did men approach her?" Victor asks. If she is a succubus, she's stunning. That's what lures in our prey.

"Oh yeah," Xavier laughs. "About five of them

approached her. I overheard one offering her money to go with him to the bathroom to suck him off." Both men start to snicker, and I tilt my head in question.

"Dude," Memphis sobers. "She punched him in the fucking nose."

"Wait, what?" I blink in shock.

"Don't really know." Memphis shrugs. "She punched him, cursed, and left. We tried to follow her, but she vamped out, so we called Salvatore."

"What was she wearing?" I need all the information I can get. It will be hard to catch her if she senses us. My idea is to find her and watch where she goes to see if I can track her to wherever she's staying, then surprise her while she is sleeping.

"Tight leather pants and a black shirt," Xavier says. "There was a beer logo on the back."

"Her hair is braided, too," Memphis adds.

"I think I know where she might have gone," Victor says. "If she's on the hunt, I don't think she's going to hide out after being here. She's going to up her game and go to someplace larger."

"Do you think she went to the club downtown?" I ask.

"That's the place," he replies and pulls his jacket tight.

There are only a few places in Nashville where someone with her kind of good looks could go to blend in well enough not to stick out like a sore thumb. If she wants to lay low, we know exactly where to find her.

Chapter 2
Ashera

The last bar was full of men who could identify me at a later date if one of his drinking buddies went missing. They'd all zeroed in on me the moment I walked in the door, and I ended up punching one of them in the nose when he offered me five dollars to suck him off in the bathroom.

I may be a blood demon, but I deserve some fucking respect and shouldn't be treated like a cheap whore.

The next place I find is more along my lines of entertainment. There are about thirty people waiting in a line that wraps around the side of the building, and the bouncer is picking who will be allowed inside. I quickly step behind a tall truck and swirl my finger around my head, changing my appearance to fit in with the upscale nightclub in the distance.

I love my real look. My blonde hair changes from braids to long, wavy locks. Instead of the leather pants and casual shirt, my body is covered with a sheer, baby-blue dress made by a fine designer. I'd seen this one in a magazine weeks ago and recorded it in my memory so I could wear it when out on the hunt.

I didn't need to check my makeup. The magic I carry makes sure it's flawless. My feet fit perfectly into the matching heels, but I need a moment to adjust from the flat boots I'd been wearing all day.

My hips sway as I approach the door. I don't look at the bouncer, but he sure notices me. I see his head turn from the corner of my eye, but I keep walking toward the end of the line.

"Hey, baby in blue. Yeah, you. You're in, sweetheart," he calls out. I smile warmly and wait for him to unclip the red velvet rope to let me inside. I try to pay the cover, but I'm waved off by the man at the podium.

Despite the thumping bass of the dance music, this place is elegant. White tablecloths drape over tables and pool on the floor. Booths line each wall to my left and right. I see a few empty tables close to the dance floor, but first, I need a drink.

The dark-haired bartender slides over my vodka and cranberry with a soft smile. He's not my kind of prey, but I can already sense his desire to take me home. If I can't find one to my liking among the other men here, I might talk to him on my way out the door.

I stand at an empty bistro table and observe the dancers. Half of the men on the dance floor don't even bat for my team. There are several who do, and I see one that piques my interest, but he's standing on the other side of the dance floor, sipping on what appears to be a whiskey on the rocks.

He's tall, his hair long, and he has piercings in his nose and lip. His sapphire-blue eyes regard me from his perch. I blink slowly and tuck my chin as if

I'm playing the shy, yet rich, college girl.

He speaks to a man next to him and breaks away. A fog machine blasts, filling the dance floor with a haze of smoke as he cuts through the dancers. My eyes are locked on his. His jet-black hair is curlier than I thought. I can see the ringlets now. He's lean, too.

As the fog rolls, I lose sight of him. I squint, but gasp when a hand lands on my wrist. My fangs grow in my mouth the moment I sense what he is. I try to pull away, but his hold is too much. Disappearing in a crowd is a bad idea, but I'm tempted. I don't know this man, and I hope to fuck he wasn't sent here to capture me and take me back to Pittsburg.

"You are not allowed in my territory, succubus," the man growls, lowering his face to mine. Despite his blue eyes, his skin tone tells me he's part Native American. We are nose to nose, and I inhale his sweet scent. God, it's like ambrosia. The pheromones of an incubus shouldn't affect me, but his does. I notice his nostrils flare as he scents mine.

"I'm only here to feed," I blurt out, gritting my teeth. "Then, I will be on my way." The male must not know who I am. I can relax, knowing he's from here and not there. I don't want to go back there…ever.

"It's not that easy, little one," he snarls, taking my hand in his as if we are a couple. I immediately see where he's taking me, and I dig my heels into the floor to slow him down.

"You're not taking me anywhere, asshole," I snap. "I have the voice of a demon. I can make a damn scene in here, then you'll be at the human's police department, answering questions in the next hour."

"Oh, you little demon," he growls as he turns to face me. We are nose to nose again, and I tighten my thighs. My pussy is wet, and I can't even explain how it happened so quickly. "You must see Salvatore before you can leave *or* stay."

"Who the fuck is Salvatore?"

"He's the boss," the male replies, smirking

"I thought this was *your* territory?" I ask him, returning his smirk.

"You should be spanked," he mumbles, and pulls me along. We make it ten feet before I yank on his arm.

"You couldn't handle this, incubus," I sass, trying to release his hold on me. He's strong; stronger than he should be. "Let me go and I'll be on my way."

"Too late," he replies, tightening his hold. "Don't think I won't vamp out of this packed bar with you in tow, succubus."

Before I can use my power to disappear out of his hold, a silver shackle clips over my wrist, and I curse loudly. Silver negates all the powers I have. This asshole knows it, and the little grin that tips the corner of his lip makes me want to punch him.

"Come on," he says, pulling me along behind him.

The moment we step outside, the cool wind blows across my skin. The sheer material of the dress doesn't protect me from the elements. I consider causing a scene, but I'm not sure that would be the best course of action since I'm not dressed appropriately for defending myself.

Being careful of the other humans in the club, he shows care with me, even though he's fuming mad. He slips off his jacket and drapes the heavy leather over my shoulders. A black Audi pulls up to the curb, and he opens the door. "Get in the back."

"Say please." I want to say something else, but he grunts and pushes me when the driver leans the seat forward.

The driver, who is the same man I saw earlier, throws the car into gear and presses on the gas as soon as my captor shuts his door. They don't speak. Neither one of them look back at me as I'm sprawled out in the seat. When the car stops at the next red light, I rearrange myself into a more dignified position in the back and remove his jacket. I contemplate throwing it at the back of his head, but I place it in the seat next to me instead.

We hop on the interstate and take off at a high rate of speed. I bite my lip and keep from making a wisecrack about getting pulled over by the police. We drive for twenty minutes and take the exit. It's dark, but I can tell we are in a more rural area outside of Nashville. I don't even have any sense of direction to tell which way we went.

The driver turns into a driveway and stops at a huge iron gate, rolling down his window to punch in a code. I try to see the numbers he presses, but he's too fast for my eyes to track. Again, I'm still wearing the silver shackles, and I don't have super speed, strength, or my magic to defend myself. Instead, I've been reduced to a five-foot-seven, one hundred and twenty-five pound female being taken to a secret incubus lair.

Fuck!

The gate opens and we drive up a small incline before the driveway dips again and turns to the right. I can see lights up ahead, and once we pass a cluster of trees hanging over the driveway, a mansion appears before us.

It's fucking huge.

"How many lonely, rich women did you have to feed off of to afford this?" The one who captured me lets out what sounds like a mix between a grunt and a laugh. The other male turns off the car and exits. My captor reaches in and pulls me out a little too roughly. "Hey, asshole! I have no powers right now. You could actually hurt me."

"You're fine," he barks as he walks me through the front door.

Inside the foyer, I see the other male now. He's twice the size of the guy who likes to jerk me around. He's older than me, making me think he's around thirty years old. His eyes are emerald green, but they look like they've seen many things.

My gaze swings to the male holding my upper arm. He's covered in tattoos, and I'm sure he was in an eighties band before he was turned. That long, black hair falls in ringlets, and the tattoos on his skin look like they are from another time, but they're not ugly. No, in fact, had we met under different circumstances, I might've tried to flirt with him.

The home is elegant. There are beautiful paintings in the foyer, and I shift nervously on the Moroccan-style black and red rug beneath my feet. To my left are two teak double doors and to my right is a set of stairs leading to the second floor. The room in front of me looks like a living room, but the walls are decorated in flowy drapery, and I see another male straightening a vase on a table by the back door. He doesn't look up, and I have a feeling he's a gargoyle who works for the incubi.

I jerk when the double doors open and another male walks out. He's dressed in a suit, and he's old enough to be my father. His salt and pepper gray hair and matching beard remind me of the sexy man with the deep voice on beer commercials.

"Come in my office," he groans and disappears.

I'm pulled through the door and directed over

to a chair that sits in front of the antique desk the older male is standing behind. He's looking out the floor to ceiling windows and doesn't turn around until my ass is planted in the seat.

"What's your name?" he orders.

"Depends on who's asking," I retort. I'm not stupid. I know my maker is looking for me, and I don't trust these males. The one who captured me moves closer, and I can feel the heat from his body through the material of my dress even though he isn't touching me. I can scent him again, and I try to calm my fucking hormones.

"Salvatore Reed." He offers his hand, and I reluctantly shake it. "The man behind you is Cassius Snow, and the one who drove you here is Victor Knight."

"Well, it's been real nice, but I should be going," I say as I try to stand up, but Cassius places his hand on my shoulder, pushing me back into my seat. "Damn."

"Who are you and why are you in Nashville?" Salvatore asks.

"I can't tell you," I hedge.

"You're hunting without permission in *my* territory," the older man snarls, slamming his hands on his desk and leaning forward.

"Yeah, about that…" I blush, feeling a bit of remorse. "See, I'm just passing through, and I was in need of some blood and energy." I shrug, hoping they'd take my plain ass excuse, but obviously they were serious about people being in their territory who don't belong.

"You still haven't told me your name," he reminds me, relaxing enough to take a seat behind the desk.

"I *really* can't do that," I hiss.

"Are you wanted?" Cassius asks from behind me. His hand touches my shoulder again, but in concern and not in anger. For a split second, I relax and feel a shiver roll through my body.

"I would rather go back to my motel, pack my things, and be out of your territory in the next hour," I beg. Fuck, I'll suck them all off if that would get me out of here without exposing who I am.

"You're not leaving here until we get some answers," Salvatore exclaims.

"Then I guess we will be here for a long time." I turn my head to look up at Cassius, but quickly turn away when his eyes narrow. The movement causes my hair to flow over my shoulder, and I quickly push the strands in place to keep my back covered.

I begin to stand again, and this time Cassius doesn't push me back into my seat. Instead, he snarls and grabs me by the shoulders. "What the fuck is this?"

I gasp and try to break free from his hold. It's no use. The other male, Victor, grabs a handful of my hair and pulls it away from the back of my neck. I hear them both let out a string of curses as my eyes water and lock on Salvatore. He is up from his chair immediately and comes to inspect.

"Who did this to you?" Cassius roars.

"I can't tell you," I say through gritted teeth. "I really need to get out of here."

"Fuck that," Salvatore says. He changes immediately from the pissed off territory leader to a softer, kinder male. His hand cups my chin gently, and his eyes change over from a deep brown to a blood red with his emotions. It doesn't scare me. If I wasn't shackled, I'm sure mine would do the same.

"It looks like a weird Celtic knot," Victor observes aloud.

"Sweet child, tell me the name of the monster who branded you," Salvatore demands, but his voice is softer, more concerned. I feel a sense of calm come over me, and I shake my head to get my wits about me again.

"If I am found, he will take me back...probably to kill me for fleeing," I whisper.

"Who did this to you?" Cassius repeats the question. Victor steps closer to me in a protective manner. Once Salvatore releases me, Cassius takes my hand and pulls on it until I turn around to look at him. He's searching the depths of my eyes like he can pull the information from my brain.

"Kieran Wylde," I breathe out, closing my eyes and inhaling Cassius's unique scent.

"The territory leader from Pittsburg?" Victor snarls, breaking the hold Cassius has over me with his incubus scent. God, he's strong, his scent unique and potent. He must lure in a lot of women.

"Yes," I say, clearing my throat and taking a step away from Cassius. "I really don't need to stay in town. I just wanted to feed and go on my way."

"Where are you running to?" Cassius asks, his voice trailing off on a growl.

"I don't know yet." I shrug. "One thing I do know is that he's looking for me, waiting for me to slip up so he can find me."

"Have you ever killed a human?" Salvatore asks.

"I killed them all the time when I was in his dungeon," I reply, shivering from the memories. "He'd bring them to me to keep me strong. I'd never been out into the real world until two weeks ago when I ran away."

"He kept you in a dungeon?" Cassius says in shock.

"Ah, yeah," I nod. "I was to be his queen after I learned the ways of being a succubus. I didn't want to be changed into one, but he forced it on me."

"How old are you?"

"I'm twenty-six," I reply with a frown.

"How long have you been twenty-six?" Cassius asks.

"Nine months," I answer, watching blood seep

into their eyes when I frown.

"He should be killed!" Salvatore yells and slams his fist on the desk. "You will stay here. Cassius will show you to an available room, and we will protect you."

"I can't ask that of you," I protest, but none of the men in the room are going to accept my refusal.

"Too late, little one," Cassius says, reaching for the silver bracket on my wrist. "You are under our protection, and no one will come for you. Now, tell us your name."

"My name is Ashera Andrews," I offer as he fumbles with the latch.

"Have you killed a human since you ran away?" Salvatore continues with the questions as I rub the spot where the silver touched my skin. It didn't burn, but it did leave a weird sensation of pins and needles where it was clasped.

"No," I answer honestly. "I stayed in the forest mostly, feeding on animals for blood. I found a man in a truck stop in Ohio for energy about three days ago, but I didn't kill him."

"Are you in need of a feeding right now?" Victor asks.

"I'm okay right now." At this point, my weakness from not feeding is making me sleepy. I will accept their hospitality for the night, then be on my way after finding someone to feed off of tomorrow morning.

"Come, let me show you to a room," Cassius says as he directs me to the staircase.

The stairs leading to the second floor take more energy out of me. I'm fading fast, and I'm hoping a long sleep will reenergize my body enough by morning. It probably wouldn't hurt to eat soon, too.

There are several doors down the hallway, but Cassius takes me to the third one on the left, opening it wide and leaning in to turn on the light. Inside is a four-poster bed with a fluffy, dark green covering. I don't even kick off my heels before face-planting on the bed.

"Thank you," I mumble.

"When was the last time you fed?" Cassius asks from the doorway. I turn my head to the side and notice he's perched against the threshold, his arms crossed tightly over his chest.

"I don't know…about a week ago. I had a deer for the blood," I say, resting my cheek on the bed. "I think I just need to sleep."

I blink a few times, and when I reopen my eyes, Cassius is stripping off his shirt and walking over to the bed. His chest is bare, and his abs ripple as he prowls in my direction.

"You can feed from me tonight," he offers.

"No," I gasp and sit up quickly. The rush of adrenaline causes me to sway, but I catch myself before I fall off the bed. "I won't feed from you, and we sure as fuck are not having sex."

"You're a succubus, it shouldn't matter," he teases, but I see concern in his eyes.

"Yeah, ummmm…no," I scoff. "I'm sorry, but your manhandling of me doesn't bode well for you fucking me tonight."

"We don't have to fuck," he says, but betrays himself when he starts to unbutton his pants. I hold my hand out in a silent plea for him to stop, and he does. "You can have some of my blood, Ashera."

"Fuck," I whisper.

"No fucking," he teases and drops to one knee in front of me. His head is level with mine, and I can scent him again. I don't know if my body will obey me and not prime itself for him when I take his vein. "Drink, then you can rest."

My fangs grow and I lick my lips when I see the vein in his neck pulse. I'm frozen; conflicted about the right thing to do. I have never fed from an incubus before, and I'm sure what I'm about to do won't taste like any human I've ever had.

I strike his neck with the speed of a cobra, hitting the vein. The rich, coppery taste of his blood slides across my tongue and I greedily swallow it down. My arms wrap around his shoulders when he stands, and my body betrays me as my legs wrap seductively over his hips. I feel the hardness of his denim-covered cock pressing against my panties. His scent swirls around me, and the next thing I know, his hands are on my breasts.

Chapter 3
Cassius

The moment I touch her breasts, she rips her fangs from my neck and flies across the room, hissing at me. "I don't want to hurt you."

"You're not going to hurt me," I frown. The succubus is nothing like I've ever seen. She's fearful of her nature, and I don't understand why she isn't accepting of my blood.

"I could kill you," she huffs. Her expensive dress has twisted around her body, exposing her long legs. The gargoyles were right when they said she was beautiful. There's something about this female that piques my interest to know more about her.

"You didn't get enough blood, Ashera," I scold. She has the scent of a succubus, and it's enchanting. I knew giving her my blood would cause sexual need between us, but what I didn't expect was for her to stop feeding shortly into the exchange.

"It's enough," she promises, her shoulders dropping. "It's plenty. I'm sorry. I should shower."

"Not until you tell me why you stopped feeding from me," I demand, walking slowly toward her. She doesn't cower from me, and I take that as a good sign, but she does watch me with weary eyes. Something about her expression tells me she's strong, but her actions tell me she's somehow wounded. "We are not going to harm you here, and you need to trust us to help you."

"I don't trust anyone," she insists.

"If Salvatore gave you his word that he would protect you, his word is good," I promise. Salvatore gave me his word about keeping me from offing myself many years ago, and he's never failed me through all of my hatred for what I am. He loves this life, and he wants me to love it as well. "Now, tell me why you stopped feeding."

"I liked it too much," she admits, a soft blush painting the tops of her cheekbones. It's endearing, and reminds me she is new to this life.

"An incubi's blood and scent is addicting for a human," I admit, immediately frowning because she shouldn't be overcome by my scent. "You shouldn't be feeling the calling toward me."

"It is. And I do," she nods, sliding to the floor. "I'm so confused. This is all new to me."

"I'm sure it is." She'd never fed properly during her time with her maker. He never taught her the ways of a succubus, and that's completely against the rules. I can't even imagine what she went through. "Please, trust us to help you."

I approach her, holding out my hand. She hesitates for a moment before sliding her fingers across my palm. I close my hand and give her a slight tug to get her to her feet. She straightens the dress and frowns at its condition.

"I liked this dress," she sighs, and swirls her

finger around her head like a ballerina. Her outfit changes from the expensive dress to a blood red robe that hangs to her ankles. "Can I have a moment to shower?"

"Sure." I clear my throat. The overwhelming urge to pull the sash to expose her body throws me for a moment. I've never met a female who intrigues me like this one. "I'll take my leave to get you some food from the kitchen and bring it to your room shortly."

"Thank you, Cassius," she says, tucking her hair behind her ear. "I won't be long."

I pull the door closed as she waits for me to go. It takes me a moment to leave the hallway. Once I hear the water turn on in the adjacent bathroom, I step away and turn for the stairs. Victor is waiting for me when I reach the foyer.

"You fed her?" he asks, his gaze darting toward the top of the stairs.

"I did," I say, reaching up to touch the spot where she fed. It's already healed, and there will be no scar. "And now, I will make her a plate of food. She's starved for far too long."

"Salvatore wants her protected," Victor says, crossing his arms over his chest. He's worried for me, and I can see it in his eyes.

"And she will be," I vow. Something tingles in the back of my mind, but I shake it off. I don't even know this succubus, and somehow, the demon that rules me wants to protect her.

I duck my head and walk toward the living room, turning left for the kitchen. Our housekeeper and resident gargoyle, Fagan, is preparing this evening's meal. He's been with us since the beginning, and he looks nervous.

"She's staying here for a while, Fagan," I announce as I grab a plate from the stack on the counter. I didn't mention anything about him adding an additional setting to our usual stack of three, so I'm surprised to see the extra plate. "Treat her as you would treat one of us."

"Aye, Sir." He nods and steps away from the stove. "May I set the table for you and our guest tonight?"

"Please set it for the three of us," I state, taking a piece of chicken from the baking pan. "Ms. Andrews will be eating in her quarters tonight. She's tired and needs her rest."

"As you wish," he acknowledges and moves the plates and cutlery to the table. I finish with making Ashera's food and grab a bottle of wine from the fridge. I'm sure she could use a little drink to help relax her after the night she's had. I should probably have a drink of my own.

When I return to the room, I knock softly and wait for her to open the door. She's back in her robe, but the sash isn't closed. She's wearing a long, silky gown beneath it, and it matches. Her breasts are more or less covered. The swells are exposed, and I have to look away before I do something that might get me punched like the man at the bar.

"I hope you like white wine," I say, setting the plate on the dresser by the door. She walks over and closes her eyes as she scents the hot plate of food.

"I do," she says as she picks up the plate. I uncork the bottle and pour her a glass as she climbs on the bed. She takes the glass of wine and sets it on the bedside table. "Thank you."

"I'll leave you to eat." I turn to leave, but I don't want to.

"Wait, Cassius," she sighs. When I turn around, she's using her fork to push around the food on her plate. "Kieran thinks he owns me since he changed me. He will kill you if he comes here."

"He won't touch us," I vow.

"He's evil."

"No maker should hold their changeling hostage," I argue. "Once you awaken, you are to be trained before being set free."

"He doesn't think so," she sighs sadly. I see a flash of fear in her eyes, and I grit my teeth in response. "Look, I don't know how long I can stay here, and while I appreciate the offer to help me, I really should be going tomorrow."

"Where will you go?" I ask. She never gave us an answer earlier.

"I'm thinking Arizona or California," she says

with a shrug. "It's as far away from Pittsburg as I can go without needing a passport."

"We can protect you here," I remind her. "Please eat. We can discuss this more in the morning."

"Thank you," she replies and ducks her head to stare at the food on her plate.

The further away from her room, the more my anger swells. When I sit down at the table to eat with Salvatore and Victor, my eyes have already turned red and my appetite is completely gone. Fagan must sense my unease and pours me a glass of wine. When I drain the glass, he nods. "I'll bring whiskey, Sir."

"She's wanting to leave tomorrow," I announce when Fagan disappears to get the whiskey from the bar in the living room.

Salvatore's hand pauses as he reaches for his wine glass. He swallows and asks, "Why?"

"She thinks she can just run away from this male," I reply.

"I have someone gathering information on Kieran Wylde for me, and I've already heard whispers of things he's doing in his territory. If they are true, we have a bigger problem on our hands." Salvatore came from a strict Catholic family. He's always had respect for the opposite sex, and I've seen him kill a human male once for beating his wife outside a bar we were at while on the hunt.

Victor rests his fork beside his plate and leans

back in his chair. He pulls his phone from his pocket and presses a few buttons. He slides his phone in my direction, and I take it in my hand. There's a photo of a male incubus. "I'm assuming this is Kieran?"

"It is." Victor nods and forks another bite of food.

Kieran Wylde is a bit older than I imagined. He looks to be around Salvatore's age, but there's something wrong with his appearance. I study his light-gray hair and brown eyes. The more I stare into those eyes, the more I realize he looks half-dead.

"Do we know of anything else he has done?" Salvatore asks.

"Nothing yet," Victor replies, shaking his head. Victor was born in the early nineteen forties. He's one of the most chivalrous males I know. It's bothering him Ashera came to us so broken.

"We need to keep her here until we know more," my leader says. "Cassius, I'm putting you in charge of watching over her. Stay with her when she goes out to feed, and make sure her maker doesn't come looking for her. When I get all the information on him, we may be going up north to pay him a little visit."

Chapter 4
Ashera

The sun casts a beam of light through the slit in the drapes hanging over the tall windows of the room I'm in. It's just after eight in the morning, and I am starting to feel the weakness from the lack of feeding. Cassius's blood held me over, but today, I need to find a human to fuck and feed from. If I can find a man in his prime, I can use his energy to last me for at least a week and a half. In doing so, I can get back on the road and head toward Arizona.

Standing from the bed, I change my appearance to a female with short-cropped black hair, and on my body, I dress in workout clothes. I add a full sleeve of tattoos, and then open the bedroom door. I hear voices downstairs, and I recognize one as Cassius.

I understand they want to protect me, but I need permission to feed in their territory. Since Salvatore is the leader of the area, I should probably talk to him. I remember seeing a gym by the motel I was using, and make my plan as I head downstairs.

"Are you needing to feed?" Cassius asks as I step into the living room I saw from the foyer last night. He's sitting on the couch, sipping on a cup of coffee. His long, black hair is loose, and my fingers tingle from remembering how it felt when I touched the soft strands the night before as my fangs were buried in his neck.

"I really do," I say. "I know of a gym in town I'd like to go to. Do I need permission from Sal?"

"Sal, huh?" Cassius asks, quirking a brow.

"Um, yeah. I like giving nicknames." I sigh and shrug. "Look, I really need to feed, and then I'll grab my things from the place I was staying at before coming back here. I promise to say goodbye before I leave."

Cassius stands from his seat and sets the empty cup on the table. A male servant frowns as he walks in, scooping it up before the piece of ceramic can make a ring on the expensive furniture.

"You shouldn't be leaving this area, Ashera," Salvatore says from behind me. I spin around, seeing the older male standing in the doorway. I can feel Cassius at my back, making me nervous. I step to the side so I can put my back close to the wall.

"Why?"

"I've gotten word about Kieran Wylde," he says, holding a folder in his hand. "Come to my office. We should sit down and talk."

Cassius follows us, entering the room behind me. I head to the chair in front of Sal's desk and take my seat. He opens the folder and removes a black and white photo. I see the brand on the female's skin before he even turns the paper around. It's a closeup shot of the same brand on the back of my shoulder. The next photo he removes causes me to gasp in horror, covering my mouth.

"No! No!" I cry.

The photo is from a crime scene. It's the woman I consider a sister, and she's lying face down behind a dumpster in a pool of blood. There are lashes across her back, and her clothes are torn away from her body.

"Do you know Iris?" the leader asks.

"She's…she's one of the call girls I worked with," I say, my vision blurring from the tears. "Who did this?"

"Some gargoyles passing through Pittsburg found her," he responds, tucking two other photos into his folder. I don't care to see them. I already know how she died. "They cleaned it up before the authorities found out, then sent the information to their leader. In turn, the leader put out the information to other leaders to notify other territories that someone is out there killing their food."

"It's Kieran," I blurt. "That's his calling card. He did that because I escaped him. I need to leave here."

I try to stand, but like the night before, Cassius places his hand on my shoulder to push me down. My eyes turn red, and my fangs grow thick in my mouth as I hiss over my shoulder. Cassius responds with the same actions. My body coils as I plan to attack him.

"You are *not* leaving here on your own," he snarls.

"You can't hold me hostage," I reply, baring

my fangs again. "I've had enough of that for a lifetime."

"*Stop!*" Salvatore bellows as he stands from his seat. "Both of you calm the fuck down."

"I'm feeding, then I'm leaving and you can't stop me!" Standing, I hold out my hand to stop Cassius from coming toward me. "Don't!"

"Ashera…" His voice and anything he has to say is cut off when I disappear into thin air, reforming behind the gym next to my motel.

The sound of vehicles greet me, and I look around for any humans, relaxing when I find none. I run my fingers through my hair and calm my features. I need to look sultry to get the men in the gym to notice me.

I'm greeted by a cute twenty-something male at the counter. He's too shy for me. So, I use my magic to find a member's name from his memory to use to get me access to the gym.

"Kathy James told me you had a free day reserved for me?" I flirt.

"Oh, yes. I just talked to her," he says, then blushes after staring at my tits for a moment. "Let's see…Yup, right here."

He hands over a clipboard, and on the sheet is the name Lily Reynolds. I sign the bogus name and give him a little wink. I make my way over to the weight rack and pick up a low weight to begin. There are four possible targets in the gym. I've already checked them out as I walked through.

The first two men pay me no attention. That's fine. The other two are eyeing me as I curl the weight and stare at myself in the mirror. One of them, a large male with multiple tattoos and mesmerizing blue eyes moves away from the equipment he's using to grab weights off the same rack. He curls his massive weight and looks up at me through lowered lashes.

I want to roll my eyes, but I refrain. He doesn't need to charm me by showing me how much he can lift. I just need to know if he wants to fuck.

"You're new here," he says after racking the weight. He moves closer to me as he hovers over my small body.

"I'm just here to check the place out," I state and curl my weight again. "My friend left me a free pass for the day."

"What's your name, sweetheart?" he asks. At least he's hot, and the beard doesn't look bad on him either.

"I'm Lily." I smile up at him.

"I'm Charlie, and this is my gym," he says, holding out his beefy hand when I set my weight back on the rack. "Would you like some help with your workout today?"

"I'd like that very much, Charlie." I use my husky voice and allow him to take me around the gym. We work out for about an hour before I'm laying on the floor, trying to catch my breath. It's been awhile since I played the role of a gym rat, and I'm totally out of shape.

"Would you like to go out for a drink? Maybe some food?" he asks as he helps me up.

I lean into his chest and give him a sexy smile. "I'd like that, but first, I need a shower."

"I could use one too," he says, looking around the gym. "I have a personal shower in my office you can use. It's much nicer than the one in the women's locker room."

"That's very nice of you."

Hook.

Line.

Sinker.

We don't make it to the shower. My body needs energy and blood, and he's all about getting my clothes off. His lips land on mine, and I raise a brow. *Not bad.* His hands slide up my sides, taking the tank top and sports bra with it. He's very good at getting it off, and I roll my eyes. He's done this before.

"Sit on that couch, big boy," I hum, giving him a little push as I shed my pants.

He doesn't hesitate to pull his basketball shorts below his ass, taking his cock into his hand. It's bigger than average, and I throw my leg over his hips, pausing to let him suck on my nipple. He gives it a little bite, and I groan when I feel the magic in my body start to swirl. The ache between my legs isn't just because of the need…I'm hungry.

Sliding down on his cock, I thread my fingers through his hair and pull his head to the side. The vein in his neck throbs, and I roll my hips, taking him a little deeper into my body.

"Yeah, baby, lick my neck," he urges. I don't need him to tell me what to do, but I do it anyway. I need him to the point of orgasm for me to put him into a trance so he doesn't fight me when I strike his vein.

"Yes, big daddy, you like that?" I moan as I move myself up and down, rolling my hips. He nods, and I feel his cock swell inside me, triggering my succubus side.

The magic I carry soothes him as I continue to roll my hips. I feel the power inside me ebb as he begins to relax. Charlie groans one more time before his head wobbles and he leans back against the couch. When his eyes close, I strike.

His blood is warm, coppery, and just what I need. I pull on his vein as I continue to fuck him. The male doesn't move now, because he's under my spell. I'm a succubus, but also need blood to survive. His hand grips my hip as his cock begins to pulse inside me. I squint my eyes when his energy seeps into my soul. I draw three more times on his vein before his life force hits me full force.

"Oh, yessss," I hiss as I release him, relishing in the feel of his cock emptying inside my body.

Charlie has slipped into a comatose state when I

climb from his body. I rearrange him so his hand is on his cock. When he wakes up, he'll think what we did was a dream. I grab my clothes and put them back on before using my renewed energy to vanish to the same spot I used after leaving Cassius's home.

I cut through the alley and produce the key to the room, sliding it into the lock. One quick swirl of my finger later, and I've changed to a forty-five year old business woman wearing a purple pantsuit. I conjure a briefcase to complete my ensemble. It takes me less than sixty seconds to gather the duffle bag that holds all of my worldly belongings, then I toss the key on the dresser, pulling the door closed. I've already paid for this room, and I don't even care to ask for a refund. I need to get to the bus station and leave town.

"Is this look called 'Susan'?" Cassius asks as I exit. I gasp and spin around, seeing the man who wants to protect me leaning against the building outside. He's wearing his heavy leather jacket again.

"Damn it, Cassius," I bark. "Why are you following me?"

"I see you found some food," he scowls, pushing away from the wall. He's decked out in all black, and the sun glints off a silver chain that hangs from his hip. He looks like a total badass, not someone who would be hanging with a woman dressed in business clothes.

"I told you I needed to feed," I huff and lift the

strap of the duffle bag higher on my shoulder. "Now, I must go."

"You are not leaving here," he responds as he comes to my side. I jerk my hand away when he tries to clip the silver bangle on my wrist again.

"I learned my lesson the first time," I say, jutting my chin out toward the shackle. "Won't happen again."

"Damn it, Ashera," he scowls and grabs my wrist. We are out of the sight of anyone staying at the hotel, and I should scream, but I can't. His touch tingles my skin, and I look at where we are connected before glancing at his eyes. The blood that tells who we are is starting to seep into them.

"Come home with me so I can protect you, please," he urges, his voice dropping with the demand.

I feel my magic slipping, and Susan is gone. I'm Ashera again, and I drop my duffle bag to the ground. He picks it up and uses his magic to transport us back to the estate where he lives. When I walk in the door, the gargoyle is there, waiting to take my things from Cassius.

"Ms. Andrews, I will take this to your room. Lunch is served in the kitchen."

"That's Fagan, by the way," Cassius informs me as he turns to head toward the kitchen. He doesn't act like my attempted escape bothers him anymore, and I curse under my breath while I follow him to where the food is waiting for us. Sal and Victor are there, making sandwiches at the counter.

"Welcome back," Victor says, stepping aside. "Help yourself. Want a beer?"

"Actually, yes," I agree, needing to relax a bit. The energy from the guy at the gym has me on edge, and I need to calm a little. If I don't, I won't be able to sleep tonight.

Chapter 5
Cassius

"Mr. Snow, will there be anything else?" Fagan asks as he turns to leave my room.

"Have you seen Ms. Andrews this morning?" I inquire as I sip my coffee. The gargoyle has stripped my bedsheets and cleaned my bathroom while I read the paper. It's been three days, and there's no mention of the guy she left at the gym.

Good girl.

"No, Sir," he replies. "She hasn't come down for breakfast, either."

"That'll be all, Fagan," I say, flipping to the financials. The good thing about being alive for three hundred and twenty-one years is that I've had time to invest some money into stocks and have made quite the profit.

Ashera is a new succubus, and her thirst is still strong. She thinks she can wait ten to fourteen days between feedings, but I know she will need blood and energy at least twice a week. She was quiet at dinner last night, and I'd bet some of my well-earned money on the fact that she's weakening.

I snap the newspaper and fold it, setting it on the small table by the window in my room. The room I set her up in is next to mine, and I did that for a reason. It's my job to watch over her while she's in our territory. I want to know where she is at all times.

With Kieran Wylde on the hunt for her, it's important she stay close to one of us. I'm sure he's sent gargoyles out to search for her, and while they are strong and loyal, they're no match for an incubus. We are demons by nature and have quite the mean streak.

"Ashera?" I knock on her door and listen for movement. When I hear none, I try the handle, relaxing when I push the door open and find her still in the bed.

She's sprawled out on her stomach, and the satin sheets are curled around her legs. They've slipped down to her lower back, and my eyes trace her ivory skin. Her curves are worthy of a Hollywood starlet, and I remember the gargoyles' words from that first night.

Their description of the succubus didn't do her justice. She's one of the most beautiful women on the face of this planet and beyond. It is as if the devil himself made her to tempt the male population of the world...*Hades* included.

I take a seat on the edge of the bed, and my movement wakes her. She doesn't speak when she rolls over, pulling the sheet with her as she goes. I can see her dark nipples through the thin, cream-colored sheet. There is an innocence in the way she looks in the morning, and I feel a pain in my chest from the thought. There is nothing innocent about who we are. The ones who changed us from human to demon did so for a reason. We are now full of sin, and we are spread out across the world to ensure there will be souls for Lucifer when the humans pass on. It's all about balance in the universe.

"Are you feeling okay?" I ask, reaching up to push a strand of hair behind her ear. My fingers tingle again when we touch, and I pull my hand away to rest it on top of my thigh.

"Sleepy," she yawns and proceeds to stretch. I have to look away, because her human body is tempting. Her scent is powerful, and I have to ignore the calling this succubus has over me. If I wasn't an incubus whose body requires the energy of human souls, I would find a way to bury myself in her body for a few hours.

Adjusting my cock, I look at the clock and frown. "You should eat something."

"I'm starving." She yawns again. "Is there any coffee made?"

"I can call down and have Fagan bring you some with your breakfast," I offer and pick up the phone next to her bed. I rattle off an order to the gargoyle and hang up the phone.

"I'll leave you to get ready," I say, standing up. I can't watch her any longer in the bed. It's too much of a strain on my need. It's time for me to feed again, and I should take a trip into town to find myself a willing woman for the afternoon.

"I'll be down later," she promises and rolls

over, giving me her back.

I slip out the door as Fagan is coming up the stairs. He nods at me, but continues into her room. Salvatore and Victor are waiting for me when I reach the foyer. Salvatore jerks his head to the side, indicating I should step into his office. As soon as the door closes, he looks up with blood red eyes.

"What?"

"Kieran has put out a call to all territories," he informs me. "He's saying she killed Iris and has put a bounty on her head."

"She did *not* kill her friend," I explode in defense, but Salvatore holds his hand up to calm me.

"I know this," he sighs. "She wasn't lying when she saw those photos. I read her, and I know Kieran is lying."

"He's going to send his gargoyles around to every territory to look for her," Victor announces as he takes a seat in front of the desk. "We can't keep her here, because I'm betting they will be on our doorstep within the week."

"Cassius, you need to take her to the cabin," Salvatore says, opening the top drawer in his desk. He tosses me a set of keys. "Pack a bag for a few weeks, and get supplies on your way out of town."

"I'll take the truck," I say, jumping from my seat. We have a heavy-duty truck we take to the cabin when we need it. The cabin was our first home, two hundred years ago when we settled in the Nashville area. Back then, finding humans to feed on was hard, but we made due. Animals will work in a pinch, but you need several large animals to even come close to the life energy of a human.

Taking the stairs two at a time, I meet Fagan at the entrance to Ashera's room. He steps aside when I make a shooing motion for him to get out of the way. The moment I step inside the door, she's changed to a sultry red head…and then she vanishes.

"Fuck!" I shout, reaching out to grab the gargoyle. "Did she say where she was going?"

"No, Sir." Fagan turns white with fear as I bare my fangs. "She only ate a little of the food, then asked me to take the tray away."

"Tell Salvatore," I order, changing my appearance and disappearing back to the motel where I last saw her.

Chapter 6
Ashera

I don't go back to the area near the motel. Instead, I try to reappear in a shopping area I visited when I first arrived in town. There are several upscale designer shops and a few eateries to choose from. I hope to meet up with an interested gentleman who's out shopping on a Saturday afternoon. If that doesn't work, I will find a bar or club nearby. Those always work.

The first place is a bust. There are two men inside, but they're with women. From my human life, I know there are very few couples who would invite a stranger into their beds. It's not even worth trying to get close to them.

The next stop is at a sports store, and I enter to look for workout gear. I don't make it to the door before I see two men, looking out of place, turning the corner up ahead. They narrow their steel-gray eyes, and I know they're gargoyles.

I push the door open to the sports store and grab a young man with a name tag that proves he works there. "I'm being followed. I need you to let me out the back of your building. If two men come looking for me, you didn't see me."

The young man's eyes widen when I produce five hundred dollars and shove it into his hand. It's something I never knew could be done, but Cassius had taught me that one night, making me promise I wouldn't abuse that power. "Right this way."

The alleyway is clear when I push through the back door. I run toward the street up ahead and slow as I reach the exit of the alleyway. Peeking around the corner, I am relieved to see it's all clear. Kieran's men must still be in the other store looking for me.

I try to casually walk down the street without looking like I've been running. I need to find another secluded place so I can vamp out and return to Cassius. He's going to be so fucking mad at me. I should've listened to him and stayed at the mansion.

I slip inside a woman's clothing shop and immediately thumb through the racks of clothes. Kieran's gargoyles are close, and I know he's on the hunt for me. I should've left town when I had the chance yesterday. I could've been halfway to Arizona, but now, I'm forced to go back to the men who promised to protect me and beg them for forgiveness.

"Can I help you?" a human female asks. She's dressed like Dolly Parton without the big boobs. Her hair looks like it hasn't changed since the eighties, and her lips are blood red.

"I'm just looking for a new outfit for work," I lie, looking for anything on this fucking rack to pretend to try on. I need to get back to Cassius's house to warn them. "Oh! This might work. May I try this on?"

"Sure, sugar," she drawls. Geez, this woman really has a Dolly fetish. "Ya know, these earrings would look amazing with this outfit. I'll set these aside and grab the matching necklace for you."

"I really only need the dress," I remind her, nervously looking over my shoulder. I don't see them outside the windows of the shop, but that doesn't mean anything. They could've sensed me and are waiting out of sight.

"Sure, come with me," she says, waving her hand over her shoulder. The dressing rooms are in the back of the building, and I say a silent prayer of thanks to whoever is out there giving me some good karma.

As soon as she leaves, I hang up the outfit and disappear, reappearing in the foyer of Cassius's home. I hear cursing and shouting coming from the office. I don't even knock, just barge right in.

Vic and Sal quiet and stare at me with anger in their eyes. It takes two seconds before Salvatore explodes. "Where the fuck have you been?"

"Kieran's gargoyles are in town and they're looking for me," I panic. "I need to leave right now!"

"We have a place for you," Vic says, coming over to take my arm in a strong hold. "Don't you dare vamp out on me, because if you do, I will shackle you with silver and spank your ass. Cassius is out looking for you now."

Salvatore holds up his hand as he lifts the phone

to his ear. I don't even need to ask if Cassius is pissed because I can hear his voice over the phone all the way across the room. He's so mad, I flinch when I hear a string of curse words coming from Sal's phone.

"Shit," I hiss. It takes Cassius less than a minute to barge into the office. His eyes are blood red and his fangs are biting into his bottom lip.

"The truck is packed and ready to go," Salvatore states as he drops his phone on the desk. "Get to the cabin, and don't you even think about leaving."

"We're not going to go anywhere," Cassius says, taking my upper arm.

I throw an apologetic look over my shoulder at the other two males and keep quiet while Cassius pulls me through the house. We bypass Fagan in the kitchen, and his eyes are wide. I try to give him a soft smile, but it turns to a grimace when Cassius's hold tightens on my arm.

"I'm not going to disappear on you," I inform him as we reach the extended cab Chevy truck. Its white and all decked out with big tires to off-road with, and I have to use the running board to climb into the damn thing.

"Don't you fucking move, Ashera," he snarls and slams the door. He's behind the wheel in a blink of an eye.

"I told you I wasn't going anywhere," I repeat, closing my mouth when he hisses at me.

I've only been afraid of one male in my lifetime, and that's Kieran, but Cassius is coming in at a close second. He's pissed, and I don't blame him. I brought this down on his territory, and he has every right to be mad.

Instead of trying to talk to him, I rest my head against the door and watch the scenery pass outside my window. There's no sound other than the hum of the tires on the road as we travel, and it's making me sleepy. The blood and energy I took from the guy at the gym is already fading. I thought it would last me for at least a week, maybe two, but it's not, and I don't want to tell Cassius I need blood. I survived on animals the first week after I ran from Kieran, I can do it again.

A hard thump to the truck wakes me, and I blink away the sleep. I glance at the clock and see it's been an hour since we left the house. The jarring of the truck is from Cassius leaving the road. We've traveled thirty feet onto a dirt path, stopping at a rusted cattle gate. He throws the truck in park, getting out to open things up. After he pulls through and recloses the gate, we are on our way through thick trees and tall grass.

It's hard to tell, but there is a path here. Granted, it doesn't look like it's been used in years, but Cassius seems to know his way through the forest. I cringe when limbs brush against the side of the new truck.

Up ahead, I see an old wooden cabin, and I'm not surprised when he pulls in behind it. I wait until he turns off the ignition before swiveling in my seat to face him. His eyes are no longer red, but his face is still pinched in anger. "I'm sorry."

"Sorry for taking off this morning without telling anyone, or sorry for the gargoyles who've come to my territory to hunt for you?" Oh, he's pissed.

"Both?" I reply, and it's honest. I don't want them to get hurt, and I'm positive Kieran will want to punish them for their role in protecting me. I'm still new to this life, but I do know that the territory leaders have rules, and although Salvatore is a fair man, Kieran's rules are evil.

"I'm more pissed that you took off," he huffs and opens the door. "Help me get these things inside, then we can talk more about how you're going to listen to me from now on."

"Okay," I reply, because that's all I really can say at the moment.

Fagan must've set us up with supplies while Cassius was out looking for me. There are several shopping bags and two coolers filled with food and water. My duffle bag is in the back, along with another bag I assume belongs to Cassius.

I wait for him to unlock the door so I can go inside. As soon as I push the door open, I frown. It's small, and there isn't much to the place. It looks like a studio apartment I had a few years ago when I first moved out on my own. There's a round table next to a long countertop. I set the groceries on the table and turn around. A queen size bed is against the far wall, and a couch sits under a boarded up window to my left. For one person, it would be cozy, but for two demons who like their peace and quiet…not so much.

I return to the truck to grab whatever's left, and find a cooler and a duffle placed at the back door. I peek around the side of the cabin and see Cassius throwing a camouflage netting over the truck. He walks over to a cluster of young trees and snaps them by kicking them. We have a lot of strength and use it to our advantage when needed. Cassius works to break the limbs off so he can use them as extra coverage for the bright white truck. By the time he's done, you can't see even a speck of the truck's color.

"Let's get inside," he says as he ushers me toward the cabin.

"What do we do now?" I ask as I enter the kitchen. He closes the door and uses a piece of lumber to board the door.

"We wait until Salvatore calls me," he replies and starts removing things from the bags on the counter.

Chapter 7
Cassius

I want to spank her for running off, but I also have the overwhelming urge to tuck her under my wing and protect her. She's new to this life, and she needs to learn the ways of our world. There's no going back now. We've been given this life, and although we hate it, we know there is no alternative. We must feed to survive.

"Well, this is cozy," she announces, taking a seat on the bed. She gives it a little bounce and nods in approval.

"We should probably talk more about Kieran and why you left," I state. She hasn't been all that forthcoming with details. "I need to know what I'm facing with this male."

"Oh, whew…well," she pauses. "I guess I should start at the beginning."

"That would be best," I huff. She's going to drive me insane over the next few days while we wait for Kieran's gargoyles to leave town.

"I was a high-class prostitute," she begins. "Well, a call girl would be the politically correct term. I was sent to an address and told I was to be there for a few days to a week. When I arrived, it was a huge mansion outside of Pittsburg. The man there treated me great. I even went to an upscale restaurant with him for dinner that night. It wasn't until about five days in when things changed."

"How?" I press.

"Well, I woke up with his fangs in my neck."
She shivers. "I guess I don't need to tell you how I
was changed, since you're the same thing as me." She
follows that up with her hand waving in my direction.

"I'm assuming he had sex with you, too?" I ask,
narrowing my eyes when hers darken.

"There was a lot of that over the first week,"
she says, clearing her throat. "Doesn't matter about
that. I'm okay, and I'm a strong person."

"Still, we don't take what isn't offered. We may
be a product of Lucifer, but even he has morals, and
taking a woman against her will is not acceptable," I
say as I take a seat next to her. "Tell me about what
happened afterward."

"Well, he locked me in his basement. I call it a
dungeon, because it was damn close. It was cold and
damp, and I had to sleep on the floor. He brought me
humans to feed from, and I was so hungry that I killed
them." She pauses to wipe a tear, but grits her teeth
and straightens her spine. "I didn't want to do it, and I
knew he wasn't going to let me leave when he started
coming to me, saying I was going to be his queen. He
kept saying he was going to force me to be his mate."

"You can't *force* a mating," I scowl.

"What is a mating?" she asks, pulling her legs
up to cross them.

"It's rare, but it happens." I sigh. "I've only

known a few who've actually found their mates. An incubus finds his mate, and it tames him, but it doesn't stop him from needing to feed on human souls."

"So, how does that work?"

"My old friend, Ellington," I begin, looking into her eyes as I tell the story. "He found his mate in a succubus, and they moved out to California to take up a new territory. There is no jealousy between him and his mate. Most of the time, they hunt together, but on occasion, they go out on their own."

"So, they're swingers?" she asks with a soft chuckle.

"Pretty much." I smile, and I realize I haven't smiled in such a long time. Ashera makes me feel almost human again. "I guess in our world, we are bred to be promiscuous."

"You are much better looking when you smile," she offers, picking at the quilt. She's young in some ways, older in others. Kieran should've never turned her, but what's done is done.

I ignore her comment and begin to pace. I need to do something to not think about happier times. My old life should've been over at least two hundred and twenty-five years ago. The only thing going for me now is that my long hair works for the current age. The early part of this century didn't bode well for me, and I had to change my appearance when I left the house to hunt.

Ashera doesn't remark on my sudden silence and leans back against the pillows. She throws her arm over her eyes, and I have to look away when the bottom of her sweater rides up to expose a small portion of her abdomen. Her body was made for this life.

"Want to help me put away these groceries?" I ask as I turn away to dig through the bags Fagan has packed. There's only a fireplace to cook with, and the only refrigeration we have are the two coolers loaded down with ice to keep the perishables from spoiling. There is a creek about a hundred yards behind the cabin that can provide fresh water for bathing.

"So, whose place is this?" she asks, taking a look around.

"Salvatore, Victor, and I bought this place and lived here about two hundred years ago." I jerk my head to the right when I hear a can crash to the wooden floor. She is staring at me in shock.

"How old are you?"

"Ah, three hundred and twenty-one, why?" I'm confused. Doesn't she know we are immortal?

"How?" I guess the answer to that is a big, fat *no*.

"Jesus, you don't know anything, do you?" I curse under my breath and pick up the can, placing it on the counter. "Ashera, we are immortal. You will never die."

"Seriously?" she asks, smiling wide. "You

mean, I will be like this forever?"

"Yes," I nod. "The only way to kill us is to starve us or decapitate us."

"That's crazy," she says, wonder coating her voice. "I didn't know."

"Kieran should've taught you that, but he's worthless and should be sent back to *Hades*."

"*Hades?*" she inquires. I find myself chuckling again at the look on her face. It's a mixture of fear and surprise.

"Yes, like hell," I inform her. "You don't want to go there. Lucifer made us, and if we fail him on this plane, he will make us suffer."

"But...but, I didn't ask for this!" she screams and starts to throw the can she's holding across the room. I use my speed to capture her hand before she can lob it through the cabin.

"Shh, it's okay," I coo. Fuck me, I've never had to deal with an upset female, and while I should be running for the hills behind this cabin, my dead heart aches for her.

"I have this need to fuck and drink blood," she sniffles. "I have all these abilities, and now I'm told I'm immortal, but don't fucking starve or get your head chopped off, because the man who created you will make you stand in hellfire for eternity."

"I've heard it's more like boiling in lava, but still," I tease, but it doesn't make her laugh. It just angers her even more.

"I'll kill Kieran myself," she snarls, her fangs growing in her mouth.

I lean forward, still holding her arm. She tilts her head back and her mouth parts. Her fangs are tiny and sharp. The memory of those fangs in my neck sends a raging need to my cock. She closes her eyes and scents the air. I can taste her succubus scent on my tongue, and it makes my cock swell even more.

"Why can I scent you?" she whispers, her eyes going glassy as if I'm putting her in a trance. "It's making me wet."

"My cock is hard for you, Ashera," I admit. We can do this, but we can't live off each other's energy for long.

"I'm hungry, Cassius," she purrs as her eyes turn red.

I push my finger against her exposed fang, nicking the tip. Her full lips wrap around it and she sucks softly on my finger, mimicking what she could do to my cock. Her eyes darken as they peer up at me. She releases my finger and licks her lips so fucking slowly I think I might find my release before I ever take off my jeans.

"Mmm," she says. Her hands are warm as they cup my face. "More?"

"Take what you need, little one," I say as she pulls me close. Her legs wrap around my waist and her arms wrap around the tops of my shoulders. There is a desperation…a need in her eyes that makes me think she's seeking solace from a storm. The strike against my vein sends pleasure straight to my cock, and I tighten my hold on her hips as I move us toward the bed. I stop and release her for a moment, yanking at the button on her shorts.

"These clothes need to go," I growl, feeling my own fangs thicken in my mouth. I will taste her body and her blood before this session is over.

Each time she pulls from my vein, my body heats and I feel her succubus powers. They're calming me, but also raising my need for her. She drops her denim shorts to the ground, and I can't take much more of the scent of her desire.

The sound of ripping fabric doesn't stop her from feeding. Her shirt and bra are nothing but a tattered mess on the floor by the time she's bare to my eyes. Her hands reach for my fly, and I tangle my fingers in her hair, making a fist at her scalp. I need her to release me. We can feed while we fuck.

My lips crash down on hers, and I taste my blood on her tongue when I swipe it with my own. She doesn't even yelp at the nip of my fang to her bottom lip. I'm stunned for a moment. The taste of her blood is pure heaven and hell all at the same time.

"I ache for you," I groan as I turn her, pushing her to the bed.

"Fuck me, Cassius," she moans, reaching for my shirt so she can pull it over my head. I shuck my jeans, and before I can settle between her legs, she flips me over and straddles my hips. When her hand wraps around my cock, I squeeze my eyes shut to keep from ending this before it begins. I haven't been this eager to sink my cock into a warm, wet pussy since I was a teenager, and the thought frightens me.

Sex has become mundane. It's the one thing I need to live, and after all this time, it's become too routine for me. Oh, I crave it. Fuck, my nature *demands* it, and I can't hate it. The rush of power taking the blood and energy from the souls I bed is too good. I don't know if I feel that way because I am a demon or if my true nature is that twisted.

Something about Ashera breathes new life into my need for the emotional attachment sex brings. I don't know if it's because I'm feeling protective of her or if it's because I'm tasked with keeping her from being killed by her maker. The more I'm around her, though, the more those lines are blurring.

Chapter 8
Ashera

His cock is deliciously thick, and the succubus part of me is craving him. It needs energy, and the blood was only a taste of what I want.

"Are you going to guide me in?" he asks, his fangs showing as he gives me a rare smile. His eyes, even though they are blood red, light up when he smiles. I have a feeling he doesn't do that often, and I should be honored he smiles for me. "Ashera?"

"Yes, I'm good," I stammer, feeling a little blush paint the tops of my cheeks. Holy hell, what am I, a virgin?

"We can stop," he presses.

"No," I growl and pump his cock twice. He forgets about my silence and leans his head back against the pillow, but he doesn't release the hold he has on my thighs.

I line him up with my opening, slowly sliding him into my depths. He's thick; thicker than most men I've been with. Adjusting to him takes a moment, and I moan when I finally take him all in. "Fuck, you're tight."

"Your cock is fucking huge," I say as I begin to lift up and slide back down.

I lean my head back as he takes over, lifting his hips to thrust inside me. The energy and life force of an incubus is indescribable. Bumps raise on my skin as our bodies heat. It's like an awakening, and the fire inside me roars. My fangs ache, and I look down at him. His eyes are blood red. His fangs are thick in his mouth, and his lips are parted.

"Do you want my vein?" I ask. My voice is breathless, and I'm surprised he even understands me.

He doesn't speak as he sits up, sliding his hand up to cup the back of my neck. I move the hair off to the side a second before he strikes. My world explodes with an orgasm that rockets through my entire body. I can't even muster up enough of a voice to scream. It comes out as a whimper, and my body tightens on his. I need him to orgasm.

"Come for me, please," I beg, rolling my hips as he takes my vein. He's not gentle, and I like it. There is a predatory growl coming from his chest, and the sound heats my body again. I don't even know if I can come again, but my body answers that for me when he jerks his head back to take a much-needed gasp of air. His lips are covered with my blood, and I immediately kiss him, tasting myself.

"Roll," he growls, pulling free of my body. I'm so lax that I let him position me on my hands and knees. He returns his hand on the back of my neck, pushing my face to the sheets, and he enters me again, swift and forceful.

"Yes," I hiss as he thrusts hard, working himself to a release. "Use me, Cassius."

My words urge him on, and I relish in the crack

of his palm on my ass. He doesn't even rub the sting away, and I don't want him to. "This is for disobeying me and leaving the house today."

"I might need a reminder of how bad I've been," I say, teasing him. I like the pain he gives me. The next time he spanks me, it's harder, and I cry out with another orgasm. I don't know if it's the excitement of punishing me, or the fact that he's finished, but I feel his energy explode as his cock swells. He grunts twice, and then he's slamming into my body, riding out his own release.

My chest aches as he fills me. Kieran punished me when I was in his dungeon, and I hated it. I hated being his punching bag when he fucked me and drank from my vein, taking all of my energy so I couldn't escape him.

With Cassius, I want the little bite of pain and dominance. The need to freely give him a part of myself by sharing my energy and blood isn't the same as when it's forced from me. This male, although a demon, has morals. He cares for me.

His cock swells more, locking us together. The demonic side of me appears, and I turn my head to look over my shoulder. My eyes are bloody. I can see the red tint to everything in the room. His eyes match mine, and we both bare our fangs at the same time. I don't know what comes over me as I pull my hair over my head. "*Mark me!*"

His body covers mine as he sinks his fangs into

my neck again, and his long hair drapes over our heads, blocking out his bite. My back vibrates from the soft purr coming from his chest. He's slowly pumping into me as he holds me in place. He's not drinking from me, and I somehow know what he's doing is more predatorial in nature. I feel my body relax when he wraps his hand around both of my wrists, pinning me to the bed.

My mind and body are his, and I feel the tingling of magic connecting us in a way that I've never experienced before. It's like a thread is being weaved, an unbreakable bond between two souls.

It's like I am him, and he is me. There is nothing separating us, and I feel at peace when he releases me, falling to the side, his flaccid cock slipping from my body. Although I'm energized from him, I am exhausted. Cassius pulls me so he's spooning against my back. This action should feel weird, because I haven't done this with any of my prey. I don't snuggle with them. Hell, I leave them basically unconscious.

"Cass," I whisper, giving him a nickname.

"Yeah?" he says as he buries his face into my neck.

"What just happened?" The sex wasn't just for our demon sides. Something happened that was monumental, and I don't know how I feel about it.

"I believe that is what happens when an incubus and succubus mate," he says, tightening his hold.

My heart freezes in my chest. All I've ever known of that word is from my captivity with Kieran, and it scares the fuck out of me.

"Let me go," I growl, trying to scramble out of the bed, but Cassius isn't having it. He tightens his hold on me again. His arms are like steel bars, and I pant heavily.

"Tell me what's going on in your head, Ashera," he demands with his mouth right against my ear.

"Kieran called me his mate," I admit, wondering why the fuck I keep opening up to this incubus. I barely know him. It's been almost a week since we met. I can't do this. All I want is to vamp out.

"Don't you even think about leaving this place," he warns. "It's important you don't go running off. Kieran's gargoyles are in Nashville, and he *will* find you."

"He will take me back and force me to be his bride." I shiver, feeling the fight drain out of me. He's right. I can't run away this time. I need their help, because Kieran will kill me if he finds me. "I don't want that, Cass."

"You are my mate, and I will not let him take you." His vow is followed up with a kiss. It's soft, and I allow myself to accept it. It's the first time in a long time a male has shown any softness toward me. I'm not used to it, but with Cassius, I realize I could learn to crave it.

"If we are mates," I start, looking up into his eyes. They've returned to the sapphire-blue of his old human life. "How will we feed?"

"We will work it out," he sighs. "Let me get a fire started before it gets dark. I'll cook us something to eat. Then we can talk."

He doesn't release me for several minutes. I think he's weighing my emotions and if I'm going to leave. I'm sure he has the silver with him, and he wouldn't think twice about holding me hostage here for my own safety. If I really think about it...I'm much safer here than out in the open.

"I'm not going to disappear," I promise, shaking my head. "I'd rather not go back to him."

"Good girl," he says, slipping from the bed. I watch as he moves about the cabin, pulling on his jeans and shirt. He grabs his leather jacket before stepping out the back door of the cabin, only to return a minute later with an armful of wood already split.

He squats down at the fireplace and arranges the wood and kindling. Within a minute or two, the flames cast a glow across the small living space. There is no electricity, and the only light we will have will come from the fire.

"Is there anything I can help with?" I ask, climbing from the bed. I forgo getting dressed and pull the quilt around my body. There is an old bearskin rug in front of the fireplace, and I take my seat next to the heat. With the sinking sun, the cabin is starting to chill.

"I'll make us dinner," he says, heading for the small counter against the far wall to gather what he needs to make us a meal.

I lay on my side and watch as he works. It'd be too easy to fall into this type of routine with him, but it's not in our cards. We are products of Lucifer. Our lives should consist of feeding off of humans and taking a little part of their souls as we live out our time here. I don't know when I will need to feed again, but I can't rely on Cassius to be my only food source.

He plates up a baked potato and a small piece of steak. He'd made two salads earlier, and I find my way over to the counter to bring the handmade wooden bowls back to the spot in front of the fire. We sit cross-legged, facing each other as we eat. I have questions, and I need answers.

"I can't keep feeding from you," I state, forking a piece of steak. It's medium rare, and I know he cooked it so I can have a little extra blood in my system.

"I know, and I can't survive on your blood either," he sighs.

"How does the mated couple you know do it?" I blush. "I mean, how do they make it work?"

"They hunt together, finding human males or females who are interested in a threesome. Ellington told me it's not as hard as it once was years ago. The humans are more open with their sexual escapades in this time than they were a hundred years ago." Cassius reaches for another piece of steak off the flat iron he placed to the side of the fire to keep warm. He holds up a piece and I wave it off. I'm actually getting full.

"That's doable." I smile and take a bite of my potato. "I mean. We have to feed, right?"

"We do," he nods. "An incubus and succubus can mate, but we are spread so thin. It isn't often you see a mated couple. Maybe I can get Ellington to come to town and visit us."

"I'd like that." I sigh, because I'm frustrated with my lack of knowledge. "So much has happened since I was turned. I don't know a lot about this life, but at least I understand what I am and what is required for me to survive."

"Let's worry about taking care of Kieran before we dive deeper into what happened here today."

I don't know how it will work. In a human relationship, having an extra sexual partner isn't as common as he believes. Orgies? Even more scarce. I wouldn't even know where to look. There's only so much a succubus's scent and magical call to a human male can do.

As much as I want to hope this possible mating to Cassius could save me from Kieran, a little voice in the back of my head says I'm putting him at risk even more now than the day before when he was just giving me a place to stay until I could move on to my next destination.

Chapter 9
Cassius

I clean up after dinner, and tell her to climb into bed. It's still quite early, but she appears exhausted and not from being weak. We've had a long day, and being on the run will take a lot out of a person, human or demon.

The revelation after our time together hit me just as hard as it hit her, but I try to keep calm. Finding a mate is tricky in our world. It's rare, yes, but it's been done. When you have to drink blood and suck the life energy out of a living human being to survive, you have to find a way to do it with your mate.

Ellington will be the first person I contact tomorrow after checking in with Salvatore. Since I haven't heard from him all day, it means things are quiet. We don't know much about Kieran, and I'm sure Victor is digging up all he can on the territory leader in Pittsburg. If he's doing unorthodox things, even for a demon, Lucifer is going to eventually find out, and all hell will break loose.

My main objective now is to not only keep Ashera safe, but to destroy Kieran Wylde in the process. The fact that he's turning innocents and holding them hostage, teaching them to kill instead of feed, is his first strike. Taking his fledglings against their will is another.

When I dry the last plate, I look over my shoulder and she is fast asleep. The succubus hasn't put on any clothes, and if I was an insatiable man, I'd wake her up for another round. Her blood is addictive, and I can't get her unique scent out of my mind. It's like sweet honey, and it's overpowering to say the least. If it wasn't for the burning wood in the fireplace, I'd be overcome with lust for her.

I add another log to the fire and make sure all the doors and windows are secure before sliding into the bed next to her. She doesn't move or make a sound as I settle in. Tomorrow, I will get answers as to why we both felt the mating pull when we had sex. I know a little about the mating of two demons, but I don't know what our future will hold.

I don't have any jealousy at knowing she will have to be with other men, and I expect her to find her own humans. They're our food. The sex is for our survival, and it's imperative we seek out strong, willing partners. I'm certain Ashera will feel the same way when I need to feed in the near future. If my calculations are correct, we should be good for at least three days. We'll have time to come up with a plan during our self-imposed exile in the woods.

As the fire cracks and pops inside the room, I roll to my side and watch as she sleeps. I rub the back of my knuckles over her soft cheek and make a silent vow to keep her safe. I won't let Kieran come for her, and if he does, I will risk eternity in *Hades* to see she's safe from his grasp.

I close my eyes and sleep, knowing the next few days will be heaven and hell.

Heaven, because she will be here with me.

Hell, because a monster is trying to take what is mine.

* * *

My phone wakes me. At first, I ignore it to check on Ashera. She's fast asleep, but stirs when the ringtone blares from somewhere on the floor.

"Yeah," I mumble as I spring from the bed and grab my jeans.

"We have a problem," Salvatore barks from the other end.

"What's going on?" I inquire and slip out the door. The morning is brisk, and I pull my leather coat tighter around my body as I take a seat on the small step leading into the cabin.

"Kieran's gargoyles killed two humans last night, leaving bite marks in their necks," he states. I hear his fist hit the desktop.

"What are the news reports saying?" If these gargoyles are sending a message, then we already know why they are here. Kieran Wylde will do anything to get Ashera back.

"They're calling it an animal attack, but there are medical professionals discrediting their reports.

The women were found on the outskirts of town to the west, and some are saying it was a coyote. Others think it's a madman."

"And Lucifer will come for us thinking we left a kill," I say, finishing his thought.

"Exactly," he responds.

"What do I need to do?"

"Stay where you are, and make sure you keep your guard up. No one but Victor and I know where you are. That could be to our advantage."

"Where are Memphis and Xavier?"

"Both are here," he replies. "They are on watch duty."

"Good." The gargoyles are masters of disguise, and we treat them well. They will kill for us, and have no problem taking orders to do so. Even though Kieran sent his own demon dogs to find Ashera, ours are loyal to us over their own kind. "We will lay low."

"Check in tomorrow if you don't hear from me," Salvatore says, ending the phone call.

Chapter 10
Ashera

We've been here three days, and I feel my energy fading. As much as I enjoy feeding from Cassius, I need human souls and blood. He voiced his concern last night as we hunted in the woods. We couldn't find anything larger than a rabbit and returned to the cabin to sleep.

Today, we will change our appearance and go back into the city, sticking to the private clubs downtown. We're risking being found, but I need to feed, and so does Cassius. His eyes are starting to sink in and dark shadows ring his eyes.

"I don't think they will be looking for us during the day," he says, using his tongue to flip the hoop in his lip. He's nervous, and I don't blame him.

"We will do what we need to do and get out of there," I promise as he leaves the cabin to remove the camo netting and branches from the truck we drove in five days ago.

It's noon by the time we reach the city, and I feel my hands start to shake. Being new to this life, I need to learn that not feeding on a schedule can cause these tremors and weakness.

I never wanted this life. It was thrust upon me by a monster. The night he slit my throat and violated me as I died will forever stay in my memories. I don't know what happened after I blacked out, but I woke up buried in a four-foot grave in his yard. I clawed my way out in the middle of the night with revenge on my mind. I wanted him dead…I still do.

I wasn't the only one. There were others; two females and one male. They were released after a month, sent home with two different men who showed up at Kieran's mansion in Pittsburg. The man and one woman left with one, and the remaining female with another man with a thick British accent. I don't know if they were sold as slaves, and I may never know.

"We're here," Cassius announces as we pull up to the valet service in front of the club. A young man in a suit opens my door and holds out his hand. I take it as I climb out of the tall truck. We didn't have anything nicer to drive, because going to Salvatore's house is off limits until these gargoyles are found.

I've changed into an Asian beauty with long, black hair. Cassius matches me with the same Asian features, and he's dressed in an expensive suit to match my luxury gown. There is a banquet for charity going on, and word has it there is a dating auction being held after lunch. I didn't ask how Cassius knew about the event, I just act like I belong as he produces two tickets to gain us entry.

"What's this banquet for?" I whisper as we make our way into the ballroom.

"It's a swinger's banquet," he chuckles from my side. I try not to show the shock on my face. *They have banquets?*

"And how did you find out about this?"

"My old friend, Ellington, invited us," he says, taking my hand to wrap around the crook of his elbow. He places his warm hand over mine and continues to walk us toward the bar. "There he is now."

Beyond the white tablecloths and fancy china, I see a man standing by a bar top. He's dressed in a suit similar to the one Cassius is wearing. It's fitted and he takes a flute of champagne from the bartender, turning to hand it to a beautiful, auburn-haired female to his right. They gaze into each other's eyes for a moment before he whispers something to her and she takes a sip.

"Ellington," Cassius says in his actual voice. He never changed his accent to match his new look, and I wonder if he has a reason for it. I now know why he stayed the same in that matter.

"Mr. Snow," his friend chuckles and holds out his hand for a shake. "Good to see you, old friend. Who is this beautiful succubus you have on your arm?"

I cringe at his blatant use of the word for what we are. It isn't a good idea to toss that around a public setting with so many human ears close by.

"Ellington Church, I'd like for you to meet Ashera Andrews, my mate," Cassius announces. I see the shock in his eyes and glance toward the female on his arm. I see a smile light up her face, her blue eyes sparkling with happiness.

"The pleasure is mine," Ellington says, taking my hand so he can kiss the back of it. "Cassius, Ashera, I would love to introduce you to my mate, Ansley."

Cassius kisses her hand in the same formality as Ellington had done mine. She holds out her hand to me and we shake. I feel her power as she gives my hand a little tug. "You're new?"

"Yes," I nod. "Less than a year."

"Dear, if you'll please excuse us," Ellington interrupts. "I have some business to discuss with Cassius. Would you show Ashera around and maybe find her something to…eat?"

"I would love to," she says, accepting a kiss on the cheek.

Cassius leans over and mimics the action but whispers in my ear, "Find someone and meet me back here soon."

"Okay," I reply.

Ansley takes my arm and turns us toward the bar. "I'm sure you'll want a drink first."

"Actually," I chuckle, "that would be a great idea."

We order our drinks and find our way to the edge of the dance floor. Several of the people in attendance are already swaying to the slow music as we approach. We don't sit at any of the regular tables, but I find a bistro style one off to the side to set my drink down. I place my back to a tall, fake shrub and glance around the room.

"See anything to your liking?" she asks, swirling the straw in her drink. "I'm liking the one with the blond hair coming in the door. Oh! Look, he has a friend."

The two men entering together look like businessmen. They can't be over thirty-five, and while the blond one is very handsome, I am more intrigued by the one beside him. Tall, black hair, with obvious muscles, because the fitted suit he wears shows every dip and valley in those arms. His thighs are thick, and he moves with grace despite his size. Two women approach him, but he makes his excuse to follow his friend to the bar.

"Come on, we need another drink," Ansley says, her eyes flashing red.

As I walk with a little extra sway to my hips, I glance to my left and see Cassius watching me. He tracks my movement as I make my way to the bar. He knows I need to feed, and I know he needs to do the same.

I'm not jealous, and from the heat of his stare, I know he isn't worried for me, either. Ansley throws a wink over her shoulder at Ellington, and we focus our attention on the two men at the bar.

"Hello," I announce as I slip between the two men. I notice the dark-haired one inhale slightly. The tops of his cheekbones darken every so slightly as he catches my succubus scent. "What are we drinking?"

"Scotch," he says, tossing back the rest of his drink. I'm mesmerized by the way his Adam's apple bobs when he swallows. "Can I buy you a drink?"

"Crown and Coke," I reply. "Thank you."

Ansley is flirting with the blond behind me. He offers to buy her drink as well. She asks his name, and I don't catch what he says. He offers her his arm, and they take off across the floor, disappearing out a side door that leads to a covered patio.

"Are you going to tell me your name?" he asks as he hands me my drink.

"Lola," I lie. I won't be with him for long, and after we're done here, Cassius can take me back to the cabin to hide out. I know he's watching my every move, and he won't let the gargoyles from Kieran's territory get to me. I'm as safe as possible here, and I relax in knowing I have someone to help me should things turn south.

"What's your name?"

"Michael Negan," he replies and mimics his friend by offering me his arm. I take it and let him lead me away from the bar.

Instead of following Ansley and her man, he takes me to a table only feet from Cassius and Ellington. The two incubi ignore us, but I see Cassius glance my way a few times as I take a seat Michael offers me.

"Tell me about yourself," he says, adjusting himself as he sits. I know my scent is driving him wild with lust, and I know he thinks he needs small talk, but I'm really in no mood. I need to feed and get out of here.

"Come on now, Michael," I purr, leaning closer to him. My hand lands on his knee and I tighten my hold. "We both know what we want, right? Why don't we skip the small talk? We're at a benefit for a swingers club, and I'm willing to bet you and your buddy are here for a good time after you make your donation to charity."

"You have a way of getting right to the point, sweetheart," he says, his voice dropping an octave as he leans in to put his lips close to my ear. "Why don't you and your friend come upstairs to the room I have with Kellen? We can all have a good time and be back in time for the auction."

"I thought you'd never ask," I reply with a husky voice.

Michael waits until I finish my drink and takes the cup, setting it down on the table next to his own. He stands and holds out his hand. I stand and use the excuse of pushing the chair under the table to lock eyes with Cassius. He nods once and returns to his conversation with his friend.

Michael escorts me through the ballroom and exits the same door Ansley and Kellen left through only moments before. He ducks into another door that leads to an elevator. As soon as we enter and the door closes, he spins me around and kisses me.

I press myself against him, feeling his hard cock against my thigh. He's eager, but I can already feel the energy inside him. My hand cups his erection, and I bite his bottom lip to drive him a little crazy. "Soon."

"I'm sure your friend and Kellen are already waiting for us," he whispers as the elevator reaches the fourteenth floor. Michael takes my hand and walks with me toward his room. It's at the end of the hallway, and when he uses the key to open it up, I am amazed at the suite before me.

Ansley is in the living room, already on her knees. Kellen's cock is down her throat and he glances in our direction. His eyes heat as his gaze travels over my body. My panties are already wet, and I feel the thirst for blood rising up in my throat. I'm parched for human blood, and I follow Ansley's lead.

I kneel next to her at the back of the couch and free Michael's cock. His hands tangle in my hair and I look up at him as I take him to the back of my throat. He pumps into my mouth a few times before cupping my face. He thinks he's dominating me by increasing his thrusts as he tightens his hands on my face. He wants to properly fuck my mouth, so I let him. It's hot, and I feel his energy start to seep into my body.

Ansley pulls back off of Kellen a moment later and giggles as he pulls her from the floor. She turns around and leans over the couch as he lifts her dress, ripping her panties from her body. "That's a beautiful pussy."

"Michael, you should do this," Kellen says, gesturing to Ansley. "We can take turns if the ladies are game."

"Oh, we are," Ansley says, looking over at me. Her expression is devious, and I give her a short nod as I lean over the back of the couch.

"Do with me as you please, Sir," I urge, taking on the title because I've already determined Michael likes control.

"Oh, you have no idea the things I want to do to that pussy, Lola." Michael pulls my panties free and drops to his knees, burying his face against my wetness. I try to hold off on the chuckle that bubbles up when Ansley looks at me and mouths "*Lola?*"

I shrug and let Michael have his fill. Kellen has already started fucking Ansley, and she's moaning with every thrust. Michael kisses my back as he rubs his cock through my wetness. I spread my legs wider as he guides himself into my body.

With each thrust, I feel my soul opening, absorbing his energy. My moans match Ansley's, and within a few minutes, the two men behind us are starting to tire. I use my power to ease Michael a little more. He pauses.

"Want me to take over?" I ask in a sultry tone.

"I have a bed in the next room," he offers and slips free of my body. I take his hand and let him lead me to the room as Ansley takes Kellen to the floor. He's still aware, and I watch her as she plays with him, riding him for a moment before she stops so he doesn't find his release right away.

"Come here," Michael orders and pushes me to the bed. He fumbles with my dress until it's out of his way and finds his place back between my thighs. His thrusts are punishing, but I don't care. It's what I need from him. He's slowing again, and I use my power to put him in a trance. My need for blood is nearing the breaking point.

"Come for me, Michael," I purr into his ear. My words of encouragement spur him on. He pumps once…twice. I feel his cock pulse inside me. Its time to get what I came for.

He slumps as he falls into my trance, but I catch his head with both of my hands. My fangs are already extended, and I waste no time in sinking them into his neck, savoring the blood I take from his body.

Chapter 11
Cassius

"Tell me about your mating with Ansley," I begin. The two women have gone off to feed, and I search the faces of the people in attendance in hopes I don't find any other paranormal beings. I don't want those gargoyles near Ashera.

"We've been together for a while," he begins. "She saved me from almost being beheaded one night in Miami. We became friends, and during a hurricane, we were stuck together at our territory leader's home. She was in need of a feeding, and since I was a proper gentleman, I offered my vein."

"Were you aware of her succubus scent?" I ask, knowing I could pick out Ashera's scent from a mile away. It was my weakness.

"Oh, yes," he chuckles. "I'd been drowning in her scent ever since we'd met. It was hard to keep my sanity around her. Now, I understand why the human males flock to her."

"What happened when you fucked her?" I press.

"Oh, my dear friend." He pauses, shaking his head. Ellington gives another soft laugh. "If you felt the threads between you strengthen and your magic pulse while you were inside her, you already know the answer to your question. Once you make love to your mate, there is no reason to seek validity of your thoughts."

"That's what I thought," I mumble, wondering where she is with that human.

"I don't even need to ask how your first sexual encounter went, because the look on your face tells me everything I need to know, friend," he states. "Ashera is your mate."

"Now what do I do?" I ask in desperation. "The incubus who turned her thinks she is his queen. I will risk *Hades* to keep her out of his reach."

"For now, keep her safe," Ellington suggests. "I have friends in some very low places. It will only take one call once I'm back in Miami to find your answers."

"Thank you," I reply and shake his hand.

"No problem." Ellington orders another drink and pushes a scotch into my hands as my eyes travel around the room.

"They've been gone for a while," I fret. I have no way of knowing where she is, and it unnerves me. Not because of her feeding, but because I don't know where these gargoyles of Kieran's are roaming in my city.

"Ansley won't let anyone touch her," Ellington says, sipping his drink. He nods over my shoulder at two women who're entering the ballroom. I feel my throat parch from the thought of feeding. "I think it's our turn."

"I do believe it is," I respond when the

women's eyes darken as their gazes land on us. We set our drinks down and head over to meet them as they cross the ballroom floor. As we near, I notice they're related, and one is slightly older than the other. The younger one smiles warmly in my direction, and I maneuver my body in a way that tells her, and every other male in the room, she is the object of my desire. It's a hunting technique, and one that works.

"Gentlemen," the one on the left says as she holds out her hand. "My sister and I are looking for some company before the auction."

"My friend and I are as well," Ellington replies, reaching for the one on the right. "I have to say that we are pressed for time, though."

"That won't be a problem," the one in front of me giggles. "I know just the place."

Before I know what's happening, we are locked in a single bathroom with the sisters. My cock is buried in her throat and Ellington is balls deep in the other one.

I have no emotions toward this woman, and I close my eyes when the revelation hits me that the only time I actually *feel* something is when I'm with Ashera. These women, the ones I need for survival, are nothing but food. They are the same as the dinner Fagan feeds me at home. There is no connection in what I'm doing.

As depressing as it sounds, I know this will be

my life until the day I die, or the day I decide *Hades* is the better option. Only now, I have someone destined for me…someone to live for. Regardless of who we are, the demons inside us rule our human lives.

Can we balance our life with our need for human souls and blood?

"Fuck me," the girl says as she releases my cock. I lift her onto the sink and send her into a trance. Ellington follows my lead and I thrust into her pussy. Its wet and warm, and everything I need to gain more energy. I feel my cock pulse inside her as her eyes close. My fangs break the skin over her vein with an audible pop. I drink my fill of her blood and release her. She sighs and slumps so she's leaning against my chest. The bathroom provides a sitting area by the door, and we take the women there, arranging them as if they sat down to take a break. I straighten my tie and leave the bathroom, closing and locking the door as we go.

When we arrive back at the ballroom, the women are standing at the bar, ordering another drink. Ashera is watching the room while Ansley has her body positioned protectively at her side. I'd talked to Ellington about our problem, and while he isn't a resident of Nashville and our territory, he came into town for the day to catch up and meet at a public place where we could go to hunt. He promised me Ansley would make sure Ashera was fed and protected while we talked.

"Better?" I ask as I wrap my arm around her waist. She nods and leans into my side.

"You?" She looks up at me through her long lashes, and although she's shifted to look like someone she's not, I can still see the Ashera I know in her eyes, and her scent is powerful.

"I'm ready to head back to the cabin," I answer her. It's an honest one, too. While I am not jealous of her fucking another man, my predatory side wants to bathe her and fuck her until that human male's scent is off her skin.

Chapter 12
Ashera

We head toward the front of the hotel. The males give the valet drivers their tickets and rejoin Ansley and I at the curb. Cassius takes my hand and pulls me close to his chest. I know it's because he is worried for my safety.

"I had a good time," Ansley says with a wink. She's brightened since our feeding, and I have to admit, it was fun hunting with her. I could see us becoming good friends if she lived closer. Maybe one day I can go to Miami for a visit.

"I hope we can do that again," I reply. I feel rejuvenated. The feeding was everything I needed, and I hope I can go more than three or four days before I have to come back into the city again.

"We will see each other soon," she promises as their car arrives. Cassius releases me so I can hug Ansley. She kisses me on the lips, lingering there for a moment. "Mmm, Cassius. She's very sweet. Take care of her."

"Of course," he responds and shakes Ellington's hand. He kisses Ansley on the cheek while his friend does the same to me. They wave goodbye as they hop into the car, and then we are alone.

"They like you," he announces, tightening his hold. I'm back in his arms again, and I rest my cheek against his heart. There is no heartbeat, because he is dead. We both are. Lucifer took our lives when we were changed, and that's the only way we stay immortal.

I've learned so much from Cassius in the short time I've known him. These things were never told to me while I was held hostage in Kieran's dungeon. How could anyone enslave another human being? All I want is for my new life to be explained to me. I want to hunt and feed without being tortured. Getting to know Ellington and Ansley today gives me hope.

"I like them." I watch as the valet arrives with the truck. He opens the door for me and helps me inside. Cassius pauses for a moment to tip the driver and starts to climb up in his seat.

A loud bang rings out, echoing in the covered parking area of the hotel. Cassius's body jerks as his eyes widen. Blood blooms from a bullet wound in his chest, and I jump across the armrest to grab him before he collapses.

"No!" I scream and pull him into the truck. Thankfully, I have extra strength, and I use it to haul him over to the passenger seat, jumping over him to sit behind the wheel. Another shot lodges a bullet in the side of the truck, and everyone around the valet station hits the ground. I throw the truck into gear and speed away, the door closing on its own from the force of my acceleration.

"Cassius! Talk to me!" I'm panicking. I don't

know what to do, and I sure as hell don't know my way back to Sal's home by driving this truck. Tears bloom in my eyes as Cassius gasps for air and sits straight up in the seat. I try to look at the hole in his chest, but I have to pay attention to the road.

"I'm fine! Fuck, I'm fine!" he snarls and pats his pockets for his phone. "Just drive until I tell you otherwise."

"Was that Kieran's gargoyles?" I swear to Lucifer himself, I will take a sword to those bastards' throats for shooting Cassius.

"I believe so," Cassius replies and punches a button to place a call. "Unless you have someone else after you."

I don't have time to even form a reply before he's talking to Salvatore. He puts it on speakerphone so I can hear what's being said. "I'm texting Ellington and telling him to get out of town as quickly as possible."

"I want you two to drive back to the cabin and stay there!" Salvatore is angry. If I didn't know he would be the first person Cassius calls, I wouldn't have even recognized his voice. "I will bring you humans to feed on if I have to until this is over."

"We will make due," Cassius replies. "I need Kieran taken out."

"We've called in a favor, but it will be a few days before we can get the extra people in place to go after him."

"We are going back to the cabin to lay low for a while," Cassius reports. "Call me with updates."

"Will do," he replies.

Salvatore ends the call and Cassius directs me toward the cabin. As we drive, he lifts his shirt and checks the spot where he was shot. It's completely healed, and I breathe a sigh of relief. "It still doesn't seem real that we heal that fast."

"Just because we heal doesn't mean we don't feel pain," he grimaces. "That still hurt like a motherfucker."

"Are you okay now?" I ask, glancing over as he leans back in his seat.

"Yes, but what energy I got today from feeding is gone," he growls. "I need you to stop at the strip club about ten miles up the road."

"No problem," I reply and continue on our journey.

"Do you want to feed with me?" he asks.

"I can," I shrug. "I'm always up for an easy meal."

We spend about an hour and two hundred dollars at the strip club. Its seedy, and with the right amount of money, anyone can take a girl to the back room for some one on one time. The woman is left in a trance after Cassius feeds. She's out cold, and the bouncer notices. We're saved when he curses and mumbles under his breath, "I'll sober her up."

By the time we reach the cabin, the sun is

setting and the temperature is getting cooler. I haul in firewood while Cassius camouflages the truck. It takes me a little longer to light the fireplace and grab a pot for a quick meal of soup over the flames. I fumble around in the small cabinet to the left of the table and find a sleeve of crackers. We sit at the table in silence while we eat. We're both exhausted from the events of the day, and although we are okay, I see the strain in his eyes.

"I feel helpless sitting in this cabin while everyone else is out looking for Kieran," Cassius announces as he takes my bowl to the small sink. He uses the jug of water on the counter to wash our few dishes.

"Do you think we should go back to Sal's place?"

"Your safety is more important," he mumbles, not looking up from his chore.

"Maybe I should be in plain sight," I suggest, but think twice about my offer when he turns to me with blood-filled eyes. "Just hear me out."

"No, Ashera," he states, slashing his hand through the air.

"We can't hide here forever," I say, knowing I'm right. "Kieran only wants me. He doesn't give a fuck about you or the others. He will kill you if you get in his way, but he is focused on getting me back into his dungeon."

"Why does he want you so badly?" Cassius

muses aloud.

"I don't know."

"Did you overhear anything else he might have said while you were there that could give us a clue as to why he kept you and not the others?"

"No," I reply, trying to sort through my memories of the last nine months.

"Think harder, Ashera," he urges. No matter how hard I think, nothing comes to mind. "There has to be a reason."

The first night I met Kieran, I was hired as a call girl. I remember my boss saying he specifically asked for me and paid an exuberant amount of money for me to stay with him for two weeks. I didn't even bat an eyelash at the length of time, because I was given a huge bonus upfront.

He was a demanding lover. I expected that, too. Any man with that amount of money and specific demands was bound to be a bit dominant. Again, no big deal.

After a few days, other prostitutes and call girls began to show up. One of them was sent home because she wasn't to his liking. The male prostitute stayed, and after the second night of being there, he was introduced to the man who eventually took him home when he awoke from the change.

The fifth night, Kieran had thrown a party, inviting his friends. I now know they were other incubi from other regions. We drank and ate expensive foods, mingled throughout the night, and once the party wound down, things turned weird.

I walked in on Kieran feeding from one of the other call girls. When I screamed, the ones who he called friends turned into monsters. Their eyes were full of blood and fangs grew in their mouths. Anyone that was human was attacked, and I heard Kieran's voice over the screams saying, "Ashera is mine!"

I tried to run away, but I was captured before I ever made it to the door. Kieran was waiting for me when his men threw me into his bedroom. I thought he was a vampire, and I begged him not to kill me.

"I will kill you tonight, and tomorrow you will be my queen," he snarled as his feet left the floor. He flew across the room and pulled me to his chest. I heard the blade as it slid from the sheath at his hip. "My master says your blood is pure enough to be my queen."

And with those words, he slit my throat.

Chapter 13
Cassius

"He said my blood was pure enough to be his queen," she gasps, coming out of her thoughts.

"Kieran said that?" I ask, coming to her side. She sits heavily on the bed and looks up at me with fear in her eyes. I kneel in front of her and take her shaking hands.

"I remember now." She pauses as a shiver rolls down her spine. "Right before he slit my throat, he said, 'My master says your blood is pure enough to be my queen.'"

"Pure?" I frown. She wasn't pure in the biblical sense.

"I sure as hell wasn't a virgin when he killed me," she scowled. "I don't even know what he was talking about."

Pure? What could be so pure about her that Kieran wanted her to be his queen, and what was that anyway? Territory leaders were not royalty to Lucifer. The only way Ashera would be Kieran's queen was in his own use of the term.

"I don't know what this means, but I should call Salvatore. Maybe he will know more." I didn't even know what to tell her to assure her it meant nothing other than Kieran Wylde was just insane.

"That's the only thing I can think of that seemed off...well, more off than the fact that he killed me and buried me in his fucking yard for a few days."

"Let me call Salvatore and see if any of that makes sense to him," I offer.

"Okay," she says, walking toward the window by the sink. I see a hint of concern on her face, and it's obvious she's thinking hard about her time with her maker.

I've tasted her blood, and it is beyond anything I'd ever tasted, but what was Kieran saying about it being pure? I'd never heard the term before, and like with all things unknown, I call Salvatore.

"Do you know what that means?" I ask, watching as Ashera moves about the cabin. Her long, blonde hair is up in a high ponytail and the ends curl ever-so-slightly. They bounce softly as she moves, and my eyes trace the lines of her hips as I attempt to keep my focus on what Salvatore is trying to tell me.

"It means Kieran Wylde is insane in the medical sense," Salvatore replies. "We don't have queens in our world. The only time a female would be considered a queen is if Lucifer crowned her, and I highly doubt Kieran would be the male our leader would pick to rule with his queen on Earth."

"He's insane," I agree. "We need to take him out of power."

"Agreed," Salvatore says, but I don't hear what else he has to say, because the front of my cabin explodes, sending wooden shards through the air like out of control missiles.

"Ashera!" I scream, flying through the air.

The scent of burning wood reaches my nose as my body falls to the ground. It's raining pieces of wood, furniture, and my fucking truck. My ears are ringing and my vision blurs. I scent blood and know it's my own, but I ignore it as I begin to crawl through the rubble. I don't know where my phone is, but at this point, my only concern is Ashera.

"Ashera!" I scream, throwing chunks of siding out of my way as I dig. I can feel shards of wood in my back, but it doesn't hurt.

"Cassius!" Victor yells as he appears where the door to the cabin used to be.

I'm desperate to find her, and I can't even muster up the words to tell him she's under the destruction. I know this was the work of Kieran's gargoyles, and I vow right then and there to find her maker and send him to *Hades* as a failure. I hope Lucifer boils him for eternity.

"Over here!" I hear Salvatore yell. I didn't even know he was here.

"Ashera," I breathe when I see her face. She's panting, gasping for air. Her angelic face is covered in blood and black soot from the explosion. "Come on, little one."

I pull the largest piece of siding off of her body, and all three of us gasp. A piece of my truck has impaled itself into her side. She curses under her breath when she looks at the damage.

"Am I going to die?" she asks even though she can't breathe well.

"No," I promise, shaking my head. "We need to get you to Salvatore's so I can take this out. You're going to need a lot of blood and energy."

"Hurry," she gasps. "Hurts."

"I know it does," I reply and look over my shoulder. Victor is on the phone; most likely with Memphis. Salvatore is at my side, and he places his hand on my shoulder when I get my arms under her body. I nod, and in a blink of an eye, we reform in the guest room Ashera originally stayed in the first night she was here.

He helps me set her on the bed, and I don't waste any time wrapping my hand around the twisted piece of metal. There is no warning, and I don't want to even tell her I'm going to do it, when I pull it free from her body.

A loud, ear-piercing sound comes from her as Salvatore presses a towel to the six-inch hole in her side. It will heal, but not as quick as my bullet wound. This may take thirty minutes, and she will bleed out until it's sealed.

"Drink, Ashera," I demand as I press my wrist to her mouth. She doesn't hesitate to strike my vein. The pain is sharp and I hiss from the sting of her fangs. Within seconds, the pain subsides, and I climb up in the bed so I'm closer to her head. Salvatore is still pressing on the wound, checking it every few minutes.

"I can't take anymore blood from you," she pants as she releases my wrist.

"Take mine," Victor says from the doorway. I move aside, allowing him to take my place. Ashera's eyes are on mine, and I reach over and squeeze her leg as Victor leans over her. His brow is furrowed, and I see the worry in his eyes. "I just fed earlier, Ashera. Take what you need."

"Energy…I need energy," she begs, taking Victor's offered wrist.

"I need to find her a human male." Salvatore curses, "She's still fucking bleeding."

"Cassius," she calls out. I watch as she pushes Victor's wrist away so she can speak. I want to yell at her to tell her to keep feeding, because I see the light fading in her eyes. "Fuck me, please. I can't wait for a human."

"As long as you're okay with us being here," Victor interrupts, moving his wrist toward her face. "You really need to drink my blood, Ashera."

"Energy, Cassius…please," she begs again.

My hands tear at her clothes. Victor moves away while Salvatore is still pressing against her wound. Blood has coated the bed, and more is leaking through the towel and his fingers. Salvatore reaches up with his free hand and rips her cotton shirt down the middle, taking her bra in the process.

Her large breasts come into view, and I feel my cock swell. Ashera's eyes are pleading, and I know she needs everything we can give her. She may not die from bleeding out, but not having blood and energy, she will wither away into a comatose state.

"I'll feed her when Victor cannot," Salvatore promises, leaning his forearm against the wound so he can use his free hand to roll up the sleeve of his button-down shirt. He's ready.

"Ashera!" I yell when her eyes start to flutter close. She jerks and awakens, but she's weak.

I pull at her pants until she is naked beneath me. I yank at the button of my jeans and push them down enough to free my cock. Her scent hits me full force, and I touch her. Her pussy is already wet for me, and I use my fingers to work her body. She needs to be built up before she orgasms so the energy she needs will help her heal.

"Pinch her nipples, Victor," I demand. "She likes a bite of pain."

Ashera throws her head back as I guide my cock into her awaiting body and Victor does as I ask. She inhales deep and pulls away from his vein, only to reach for Salvatore's wrist when he offers it. "The bleeding is slowing."

She's already taking some of my energy. Her pussy tightens on my cock as I thrust, and I swear I can't keep my eyes off of hers. The more I think about what happened, the more I want to deliver

Kieran and his goons to *Hades* myself. I will go down with them as long as she is still alive.

"Come on, Ashera girl. Take his energy," Victor urges, leaning over to take her nipple between his teeth. She snarls and growls as he delivers little bites of pain. She likes it, and as sadistic as it sounds, I'm loving seeing her in the depths of her passion.

"She's healing," Salvatore informs me as he removes the towel from her side. I've already noticed the gashes on her face start to fade, only the blood staining her skin. "Finish her, Cassius. Give her what she needs."

My thrusts are punishing, but I never take my eyes from hers. She's drinking from Salvatore's wrist, but she never closes her eyes. In this moment, we are one. The other two men are no longer in the room. I silently urge her to give me her release so I can give her my life force. If she needed it all, I would gladly lay it at her feet just to see her unharmed.

My thumb finds her center, and I rub her clit slowly, watching for signs she is needing more. The succubus beneath me is slowly weaving a web between us, and I tear my gaze away to look at Victor and Salvatore. From the worry on their faces, I know they'd die for her too.

Chapter 14
Ashera

I feel his energy soak into my soul as he orgasms, his seed pumping into my body. Victor and Salvatore pull away as they check the wound at my side. Cassius tucks himself back in his jeans and climbs in beside me, taking the spot where Victor once was.

"Thank you," I sigh, looking at my side. The hole is gone and the bleeding has stopped.

"Are you strong enough for me to bathe you?" he asks, tucking a strand of hair behind my ear.

"I think so," I say with a nod and sit up. The bed is covered with blood, reminding me of a surgery scene from a movie I once saw. "I'm so sorry, Sal!"

"This is not your fault," he growls. "The bed can be replaced…you cannot."

Salvatore leans over and kisses my forehead. I nod and accept the same from Vic. Both men leave the room with their shoulders slumped. I know I took a lot of their blood, so they're going to have to find a few humans to replenish their own supply.

"You need to feed," I scold, reaching up to touch Cassius's cheek. Dark circles have formed around his eyes and his color isn't as tan as usual. "I can bathe myself."

"No," he says, shaking his head. Something in Cassius has changed over the last hour. It could very well be the excitement from the explosion, but I think it's something else. "I will care for you."

"Okay," I say, letting him carry me from the bed. Halfway to the bathroom, he stumbles.

"Put me down," I order, throwing my hand out to catch the doorframe. He's being stubborn, and I won't have him trading places with me just so he can be chivalrous.

I shimmy out of his hold, and this time he doesn't protest. He leans against the bathroom sink while I turn on the spray in the walk-in shower. There's room enough for four people. So, it's no hassle when I step inside and watch him as he removes his clothes.

His long, black hair is still full of debris, and I turn to push him under the water as soon as he closes the glass door. I work the strands of his hair while he shuts his eyes. Instead of him caring for me, I am cleaning the day's events off of him. Pieces of wood flutter to the shower floor, washing down the drain along with the fear of the explosion.

Kieran is out to get us all now. We thought hiding in the cabin would keep me safe while Sal and Vic hunted Kieran's gargoyles. I should've known they'd find me. I'd used the few days alone with Cassius as a way to hide from my problems. The fairytale I'd conjured in my mind was fun while it lasted, but I've never been one to run from a threat.

"Kieran needs to die," I say as I work the

shampoo into Cassius's hair.

"I will torture him before I kill him for the things he's done to you," he vows, but his voice holds no strength. He's weakening from feeding me during my injury. As much as I appreciate all three of them helping me, it's not healthy for an incubus to share their resources with a succubus.

Regardless of what's happening between Cassius and myself, we are demons. We must have humans to live. There will never be a time when we can feed off of each other and live happily ever after. That's not how we work.

"I want you to go out and feed," I whisper and cup his face. His eyes are his normal sapphire-blue, and I stare into them for several seconds before taking his lips in a soft kiss. The silver hoop in his lip is warm to the touch, and I nibble on it before stepping aside. "Get dressed and hunt with the others. I'm sure Memphis, Xavier, and Fagan can hold things down here until you return."

"Let me bathe you," he argues, turning me so I am under the showerhead. Warm water cascades over my body, and I look at my feet to see the remaining blood swirl around the drain before disappearing.

His hands roam my body and I feel an ache between my legs. His scent is overpowering as I lean into his embrace. My lips touch the spot over his heart, and I just stand there as he holds me. We don't talk, and that's okay. I need to take stock of what happened. I've never been seriously hurt like I was earlier, and for once, I'm thankful for my immortality.

"You should go, Cass," I whisper and release him. He nods, kisses me softly on the lips, and pushes the door open. I don't even watch him as he goes. I just tuck my head under the water and bathe myself.

By the time I am done, I make my way next door to my usual room. The bed in the room I'd been using is destroyed. Cassius's room is as plain as the other ones. There are no personal items laying around on the dresser, and not one photo on the wall belongs to him. If he hadn't told me he'd been with Sal for such a long time, I would've thought he was newer to this life than I am.

Even with the energy I took from Cassius and the blood that filled me from all three of them, I am exhausted. His bed smells like him, and I find peace and comfort between the sheets when I slip beneath them.

I turn on the television and hope the soft hum of voices will lull me to sleep. I don't know how long he will be, but I do know we both need our rest. Plans for Kieran's death will need to be addressed in the morning. I don't know if they have any idea how to get to him, but I do. I know I have to walk back into the dragon's lair and face the demon who made me. At this point, it's the only way.

I know I promised Cassius I wouldn't run, but

I'm going to have to break that promise and head back to the one place I swore I'd never return.

Chapter 15
Ashera

Slipping from the bed, I use my magic to give myself an outfit since all of my clothes were destroyed in the explosion. As easy as it would be to conjure up a look for each day with nothing more than the swirl of my finger, I like to keep some sense of my human life by shopping and dressing myself.

Cassius came in a few hours ago, and I heard him take another shower before he came to bed. His incubus scent was strong after his feeding. He spooned me as he settled in, but I didn't speak. All I wanted to do was sleep, knowing everyone was safe under Salvatore's roof.

I never left the room last night to check on Sal or Vic. I heard voices at one point, but I couldn't muster up enough energy to even go downstairs for a quick meal before I fell asleep.

The door barely makes a sound as I close it softly. I twirl my finger around my feet to apply a comfortable pair of jogging shoes to go with my workout clothes. Its comfortable, and I'm really in no mood to dress up for the mission I'm about to embark on before the end of the night.

"Ms. Andrews," Fagan calls out as I enter the living room. He's cleaning the furniture again…just like he does every morning. "Fresh coffee is available, and I will serve breakfast at nine."

"Thank you, Fagan." I nod and pass him to find the kitchen empty. Sal and Vic are nowhere to be found, and I breathe a sigh of relief. My goal is to sit down with a hot cup of coffee outside so I can make my plan. It'll need to be a solid one, because I'll only get one shot at taking out Kieran Wylde.

"Good morning," one of the gargoyles says as he enters the kitchen. I remember him from somewhere, and I narrow my eyes. The tall, tattooed man smirks and pours himself a cup of coffee. "Yeah, yeah. I know. You saw me at that sleezy bar."

"I did," I reply and take a sip.

"Well, you were in our territory, and I needed to keep an eye on you," he says and leans against the counter. He's a little on the beefy side, and I notice a small scar over his left eye. His short, brown hair is shaved close at the sides, and he has a flower tattooed on the side of his head. If he grew out his hair, you'd never know it was there.

"And look where that got me," I mumble and take a seat at the breakfast bar in the middle of the kitchen.

Another gargoyle enters the kitchen and mumbles some sort of greeting. He's the same size as the last one, but he's only wearing a pair of basketball shorts. They ride low on his hips, and I watch as the muscles in his back ripple with his movement.

"I'm Memphis, by the way," the first one says, taking the empty seat to my left. "The quiet one is

Xavier."

"Nice to officially meet you," I reply. My eyes are still locked on Xavier. If he was human, I might use my powers to feed off of him, but I know gargoyles aren't to be used as our main food source. They're sent here to be our slaves, our helpers. However, nothing says they can't give us some of their energy and blood when we are in need.

"Salvatore is still out hunting," Memphis informs Xavier when he turns around, resting his ass against the counter.

"Victor?" he asks, his eyes still downcast as he drinks his coffee.

"He's up, but hasn't left his room yet," Memphis states with a shrug. "I heard the shower going when I left my quarters."

"Cassius didn't return until five this morning," I add.

"Heard you had quite the accident yesterday," Memphis teases.

"Seems I'm a target," I reply, smiling for once since the explosion. "They missed, though."

Both men chuckle. Even Xavier looks up from staring into his cup. Fagan enters and quietly rummages in the cabinet for a few pans. He shoos Xavier from his spot by the stove and gets down to making a full breakfast, mumbling something about feeding us a real meal.

Fagan offers to refresh my coffee, and I let him,

because it appears he isn't real happy about sharing his kitchen space while he's cooking. Xavier leans his hip against the island and stares down at me. We're only six inches apart, but he still towers over me.

"If you're not with Cassius, I will be your guard," he grunts. His voice is super deep, and it holds an air of authority I like in a male. It's strange, having a gargoyle demanding your safety. We're supposed to be strong enough to take care of ourselves.

"I think I'll be okay on my own," I press. The gargoyle raises a brow at me, and begins to speak, but he looks over my head instead.

"I asked him to be your protection if I couldn't be there," Cassius says from the doorway.

"I don't need protection," I say, gritting my teeth. "You see how well that worked the last time, didn't you?"

Cassius's eyes turn red as he stalks toward me. I'm not going to let him intimidate me. "I'm not running away anymore, Cass. It's time we go to Pittsburg."

"Absolutely not!" he roars and bares his fangs. I don't even flinch as I cross my arms in defiance. "If he gets you back in that house, he's going to punish you…torture you, Ashera. When he's done with you, you'll be begging for eternity in *Hades*."

"Not if I remove his head first," I huff and jump off the barstool. I glance around the kitchen and see the two gargoyles are missing. Only Fagan is left, and he is too busy cooking to pay attention to our argument.

"Are you planning on leaving?" Cassius gasps, narrowing his eyes. "I will shackle you, again."

"I don't think so," I yell and disappear into thin air. The last thing I see is the look of fear on Cassius's face.

When I reform, I'm in a shady area of Pittsburg; my old stomping grounds. I know where I need to go to acquire a blade for my mission. I need one that's easily concealable…and sharp.

The bell over the door chimes with my arrival. A man behind the counter folds his paper and looks up at me over the rim of his reading glasses. His eyes narrow before he gasps and jumps to his feet. "Ashera! Where the fuck have you been?"

"I…um." Fuck, I didn't think about an excuse before I came. Henry hasn't seen me in almost a year, and I'm sure he has questions. "I left town to find a better job."

"Wait, really?" he asks, his voice full of surprise.

"I'm living down south now," I offer as an answer. "I like the warmer weather."

Henry chuckles and comes around the counter to hug me. I try not to let his affection get to me. When I was human, he was all I had. If it wasn't for my cousin, I wouldn't have made it living on the streets. He gave me a place to stay until I found the job at the call service. Granted, being a call girl paid better than a prostitute on the streets, and I got nice perks. Sometimes, the men I serviced paid me above what the fee was for my time.

"We've had people in here looking for you," he informs me. *Fuck! Fuck! Fuck!* Kieran's gargoyles must've found out my information through the call service. My maker knows more about me than I expected.

"Henry, you need to leave town," I growl. "It's not safe for you to be here for a while."

"I'm safe, Ashera," he assures me, nodding toward a shotgun behind the counter. "It's you I'm worried about."

"I'm fine," I promise. "I'm going to be fine."

"What's going on? Why are these men looking for you?" He's concerned. I can see it all over his face. I can't just tell him I'm a demon now. First of all, he wouldn't believe me, and secondly, I don't need anyone from my past life put in danger.

"Henry, I need a weapon," I admit. I could've just magically produced one, but I wanted to see him one last time. I needed to make sure he was okay. I know I'm punishing myself by visiting humans from my past, but Henry is special to me. He will *always* hold a special place in my heart. "Please don't ask me why. I need a knife…one that's at least nine to twelve inches long. Something I can hide in my clothes."

"Ashera," he begins, but I slash my hand through the air to stop him from getting emotional.

"Look, if you don't help me, I'll go somewhere else," I explain.

"No, I will help you, but you better not get arrested or die." He huffs and removes his glasses, setting them on the display case.

"I'll be careful," I lie. I don't need him knowing what I'm about to do.

Henry removes a long knife from the bottom of the case. The handle looks like it's made of some type of bone, and its blade appears to be sharp. That's exactly what I'm looking for.

"Do you even know how to handle one of these?" He hesitates before he hands it over, and I take it from his hand before he can put it back in the case.

"Well, yeah," I scoff. It can't be that hard, right? Just put the blade to his throat and cut. That's all I need it for, and after I'm done, it will take a long swim in some deep water.

"You're worrying me, Ashera," he finally says after I take the blade and tuck it in the back of my pants, then tuck the handle up under my bra. I'm wearing a hoodie because the weather in Pittsburg is much colder this time of year than it is in Nashville. With my bulky clothing, the knife is concealed well.

"I don't want you to worry, Henry," I whisper and fight back tears. I throw my arms around his neck and squeeze him tight. "I need to go."

"You better not ghost out on me again," he warns and points his finger in my direction. "You're the only family I've got, little lady."

"And you're all I have," I sniffle and pull the door to his shop open wide. I can't look back at him, knowing I probably will never see him again. It's best he goes on with his human life and doesn't worry about me anymore.

I have a new life, and one I hope I can continue in Nashville with Cassius. My life is different with him. There is a thread that binds us now, and I know he is the man to own my dead heart. Love was something I'd dreamed about when I was a human.

Oh, how things have changed.

Once I'm around the side of the building, I check for any humans. When I find none, I disappear out of sight and change locations. I'm surprised to see the call service is out of business and there is a sign in the window saying the place is for sale. I peek in the windows and see nothing left of the front office. There's not even a speck of the old green carpet on the floor.

I realize my old life is gone. There is nothing left to salvage here, even if Kieran is dead. My soul aches for Cassius, and I should've waited for their plan to be put in place. But it's not fair for them to risk themselves to take care of what is mine to destroy.

I need to kill Kieran, and it's time I take him out. I return to the alley behind the building and look around for any sign of humans. There is a sound up ahead. I'm sure it's one of the homeless men who sleeps behind the dumpster. I hesitate before I vamp out just in case it's not.

A silver chain wraps around my throat, and I kick out when my captor starts walking backward, causing my feet to drag on the ground. I'm helpless and can't use my powers to escape.

"You little whore," a gargoyle growls at my ear. "Kieran is looking for you."

My hand slides up the back of my hoodie, and my fingers wrap around the handle of the knife. I may not be able to disappear, but I can still defend myself.

I roll my body so I am facing the gargoyle. His eyes go wide when I stab him with the knife, pushing it all the way to the hilt. Warmth spreads over my hands, and I push his body away as I remove the knife.

"Tell Kieran I'm coming for him," I snarl and yank at the silver on my neck. The gargoyle has wrapped it around me, and there are tiny razor-like points in the wire. I hiss as I try to pull it away, but when I unstick one sharp point, another imbeds in my skin.

The gargoyle is moving around now, and I take off at a dead run down the alleyway. It stretches the block, and I can see a road up ahead. When I look behind me, he's on his feet, healed from my attack.

I can't drop the knife, nor can I replace it in my clothing as I run. I need to find help, or at least a human who will stop when he sees a helpless female running from a bald thug with tattoos and a peacoat.

I'm feet from the road when a gun goes off and I am knocked to the ground. The pain in my back is nothing compared to the inability to feel my legs. I'm numb. There is nothing below my waist, or at least the sensations are missing. I know he's shot me directly in my spine. Whatever he shot me with, it worked to his advantage. I scream when I realize I am paralyzed and can't heal due to the silver chain imbedded in my neck.

I crawl with my arms, but I can't make it to safety no matter how hard I try. The sound of footsteps gets closer and closer the more I try to struggle. My breathing is starting to fade, and the silver around my neck keeps me from at least starting to heal my body.

"You fucking cunt!" The gargoyle rears back with his booted foot and kicks me in the jaw. Stars bloom in my vision, and I blink to keep myself aware, but it doesn't work. He kicks me again, but this time, everything goes dark.

Thick fangs in my neck wake me. My eyes blink to clear the confusion, and it takes me several seconds to realize I'm on my back, staring at a ceiling I remember. I'm weak, but alive…for now.

His stench is overpowering, and I feel tears leak from the corner of my eyes. There are no sensations below my waist, and right now, I am thankful. Without feeling, I am numb to everything he's doing except drinking from my vein.

Taking my blood, I can handle. That's nothing compared to what else he has in store for me. My only prayer is Cassius finds me in time. I don't want a real death. I want to live, and I want to live eternity with my incubus mate.

I bring up a picture of him in my mind. I need to see his smile to remind me there is good in the evil of our lives. Demon or not, I love him, and I will serve my time in *Hades* if Lucifer sees fit. I will accept my fate even if I don't agree with it. At this point, I have nothing else to hope for if Cassius doesn't come. I am a vessel for my maker, and he will make me suffer before killing me.

"Oh, my queen, how I've missed you," Kieran growls as he rips his fangs from my neck.

His eyes are blood red; my energy is now his. There isn't anything more for me to do other than shut down. It's time to close myself off to the world and pray I'm killed quickly. My brain goes dormant, protecting itself, as I close my eyes and fade away.

Chapter 16
Cassius

Every part of my body is on fire. They've taken Ashera from me, and I'm on edge without her by my side. Victor paces the room, and I want nothing more than to take my anger out on him. The demon inside me wants blood, and I won't stop until Kieran Wylde is burning in *Hades*.

"Memphis is bringing more gargoyles," Victor announces after looking at a message on his phone.

"How many?" I ask, my voice flat.

"Five," he replies and continues pacing. Memphis left before dawn, stating he was going to gather help. I didn't want to wait, but his argument was valid. If I'd gone in there with the anger of her kidnapping, I was bound to get us all killed.

As much as I hated my extended and immortal life, Ashera has giving me a reason to live again. If anyone could tame the incubus inside me, it's Ashera Andrews. Over the past few weeks, my disgust at living hasn't been at the forefront of my mind. Feeding isn't as depressing as it once was, and I owe it all to her.

Even though I've only heard of a handful of matings, I know it isn't all hearts and fucking flowers like the human marriages. Being demons, we need sex and blood to survive, and living off of your succubus mate won't keep you alive for long. We *must* find willing bodies, and jealousy isn't a part of our essential makeup. The only anger we posses is when our mates are taken against their will.

I won't allow Kieran to harm her again. It's no secret he violated her and slit her throat to change her. I will kill him for that alone. We don't know the others who were changed that night with Ashera, but I'm betting he did the same to the women and possibly the man.

"They're here," Victor announces and heads toward the door.

I've been in a trance. My body has basically shut down, storing its energy reserves for the impending war. I should feed again before we leave, but I don't have time to hunt for a human. It's too important I get to my mate.

Memphis enters with five gargoyles, and I blink when two of them are women. Victor makes the introductions, and I try to keep up. They're from the Washington D.C. area, and one of them is Xavier's brother. Their territory leader, Caspian, sent them as soon as Salvatore called in a favor. What that favor was, I don't know, nor do I care at this point.

"Shai, Roan, and Laran will be going with us," Memphis says as he takes charge of our mission. I'm too lost without Ashera, and I cannot think about anything other than finding her and bringing her home.

"Laran brought you two of their gargoyle

females for energy and blood," Xavier says, nodding toward the two females. "Briley and Lacey will be available should any of us need it." Gargoyles survive on blood alone, and fortunately for them, they can feed on their females and survive.

"Thank you." I nod, knowing I may need them once this is over. The three other gargoyles stand at attention against the wall. Victor speaks to them as he gives them the plan. I'm ready to go. I don't want to wait much longer.

"We know the area well," Laran informs us. I try to listen as he explains the area, but the more we wait, the more my body begins to tremble. "The mansion is surrounded by forest. It's going to be easy to reform in a hidden area I remember seeing not far from the back entrance to the home. He has four gargoyles who care for the property and four incubi on his payroll."

"Where are they keeping Ashera?" I ask. That is the only question I need answered.

"The basement dungeon can be accessed from behind a bookcase in his office," another gargoyle answers. "I can get us down there."

"What are we waiting for?" I growl and reach for my jacket.

The gargoyles explain the layout of the home to Xavier, so I head toward them. It's time to go, and I'm going to figure out how to transport there by myself if they don't get ready to go in the next two minutes.

"You need to calm the fuck down," Victor says as he grasps my elbow. I feel my fangs extend, and I bear them in his direction. Before I can say anything, his eyes darken and blood seeps into the whites of his eyes, causing vein-like streaks. "We don't need you going off all half-crazed. You're having withdrawals from not having Ashera here, and you need to recognize that is a sign of not having your mate close. I know you have no idea about incubi matings, but this is a fucking sign. If you don't get it together, I will silver your ass and leave you here."

"There's no fucking way you are leaving me here," I snarl.

"Everyone gather around," Xavier announces.

I jerk my arm out of Victor's hold and stand next to Memphis. The three other gargoyles stand in the center of a circle we've created, and we place our hands on their shoulders. I blink, and I'm standing just on the edge of a forest-like area, looking across a small clearing. Beyond that is a home as large as the one we have in our territory. There are no guards, no one ambling around. There are two cars in the circle drive, and from the looks of it, things are quiet.

I close my eyes and use my enhanced hearing to try and listen for Ashera, but it's quiet. I don't know if I should take that as a good sign since we know she's in the basement of the home. She told me of the things he'd done to her while she was captive once before, and I fear he's already touched her.

He's touched what's mine.

Mine.

Mine!

"I'm going in," I growl.

"Cassius, no!"

Too late. Their voices fade as my body disintegrates into thin air. I transport myself across the lawn, reforming at the back door. One well-placed kick to the glass pane and it shatters. My body has swollen; my fangs are present. Claws have erupted from the tips of my fingers, and I know my face has taken on its demon state.

Two gargoyles come around the corner and attack. Laran and Xavier are on them before I can take them out myself. My taste for blood is at the forefront of my mind. I don't know where this office is, but I will tear down this house with my bare hands to find her.

"Go!" I hear Memphis behind me. Victor places his hand on my shoulder, silently telling me he has my back.

An incubus appears in the hallway, his expression similar to my own. His eyes are black with fury, but I am running on anger. He rushes me, but I slash my claws against his throat until blood spews out of him and he gasps for air. Victor catches him when he falls, and twists his head until it comes clean off his body.

"Turn right," one of the gargoyles calls out as we continue. Ahead of me is a living room and another hallway. Shai points toward the hallway and presses his finger to his lips, telling us to go quietly.

There are doors on each side of us, and Laran holds out four fingers, then points with one of them to the right, telling me that's our destination. I pause to listen, and when I hear nothing, I take a deep breath and move on. When I reach the door, I try the handle and it opens softly.

"Be aware," Victor warns. "It's too quiet."

"Well, well, well," a voice says from my left as soon as I enter. "Come for my whore, Cassius?"

"She's not your whore," I snarl. I don't even recognize my own voice. Seeing Kieran Wylde at his desk with Ashera on her knees, collared like a dog, sends me into a feral rage.

"Ah, ah, ah," he tsks, producing a hunting knife and pressing it to her throat. "If you even think about killing me, I will send your bitch straight to *Hades*."

"I'll kill you if she dies," I shout. There is a silver shackle around her upper arm, stripping her of any power she might've had to escape him.

"And I will have her for eternity," he laughs.

Ashera looks straight ahead. There is no emotion in her gaze, and I swear she's looking right through me. She isn't even aware of my presence, and that scares me. I take a step forward so I can see her better, but Kieran presses the blade harder against her neck, nicking her skin. A lone trail of blood appears, rolling down over her collarbone and onto her naked breasts. I do everything in my power not to rage when I see healing bruises all over her body. There are scabbed-over knife marks on the tops of her legs and forearms. With our healing abilities, they have to be only an hour old.

What else has he done to her over the last twelve hours?

"Here's what's going to happen," Kieran begins. "You and your merry bunch of assholes are going to leave my house before we kill you."

"I'm not leaving until I have Ashera and you are burning in hell," I reply.

"Not going to happen," he says, taking the knife and running it across her neck, cutting only a few layers of skin. It's enough to bleed, and she still doesn't respond.

Behind me, I know Victor is to my left and Laran is to my right. Directly behind me is Xavier, but I have no idea where Memphis, Shai, and Roan are, and I hope Kieran doesn't realize there are more of us.

"Release her," I demand, taking a half step to the right.

"She's mine," he insists. "I made her, so she belongs to me."

"She's my mate, asshole," I snarl. "She belongs to me."

There is a silence that falls over the room. My face bubbles with anger. Ashera still isn't reacting to anything, and I fear she has completely shut down. My beautiful mate will have to be saved. There is no way she will be able to fight her way out of this.

"I guess we both want that pure blood," he states.

"Whatever you're jabbering about is nothing," Victor snaps from beside me. "There is no such thing as a pure blood succubus."

"Oh, I beg to differ," Kieran chuckles and stands. He pulls on the leash and Ashera stands. She is completely nude and the blood from the cut to her throat has now reached her belly. Little drops roll off the ends of her nipples, and I can scent her from across the room. Her succubus scent is alive, and it gives me hope. She still stares at me, but it's blank.

"How so?" I ask, jutting my chin toward Ashera. "What is so special about her that you kept her chained to your dungeon for nine months?"

"You really don't know?" he gasps. "You really are fools. You don't deserve her."

This incubus is working on my last nerve. As soon as I find an opening, I will go for his throat. This kill belongs to Ashera, but she is in no shape to react. The silver prevents her from defending herself. She can only rely on her human strength, and that is no match for a demon.

Nine months. Nine fucking months she was

chained in that dungeon and subjected to his sick pleasures. Even among demons, we have rules and standards. Never take more than you need, and never force yourself upon your food.

Never.

How she managed to stay sane in the time she spent with him, I will never understand. Nine months is a long time to be chained and violated. He'd fed her with humans, demanding she kill them. He wanted her fed, and you'd think he was caring for her for those…nine…months.

"You wanted to breed her!" I roar, my body vibrating with anger. "She's a pure blood because she can still have children?"

"Took you long enough," Kieran says, rolling his eyes. "The first time I tasted her, I knew. There have only been a few before her, and they all come from the same bloodline. You see, your mate here is a queen of our race, and a queen among the succubi. She will hold power over the world, and I made her specifically to help me rule."

"She is not your queen, nor will she ever be," I remind him.

"Unfortunately, she wouldn't bear a fucking kid during those nine months," he spat. "Even when she was fertile, I couldn't impregnate her. She's worthless. I should've just killed her, but I need her bloodline."

"It's probably because you can't perform

enough to impregnate a female." I taunt him. I know I am, but I need him to pull the knife away from her throat and come at me. I want to make him so raging mad that he releases her. "Your cock just ain't what it used to be, huh?"

"Are you shooting blanks in your old age, Kieran?" Victor teases, taking my lead. Victor and I have been friends for so long, we sometimes know what the other one is thinking, and I'm thankful now is one of those times.

"Fuck you," Kieran snarls. I see the blade ease away from her neck. I wish I could communicate with her and tell her to run when I attack him, but even pleading with her by a look alone isn't working. She's still as a statue.

"How do you even feed?" I continue. The knife drops another half of an inch, and I feel my body wanting to coil for the long jump across the room. I'm primed, and I will get my mate if it kills me.

"With my fangs buried in your whore," he answers, setting me off.

The muscles in my legs coil, and I fly across the room. I make impact with Kieran as he yanks the blade across Ashera's neck. My guttural cry echoes throughout the room as voices explode behind me.

"You bastard!" I yell as I wrap my fingers around his throat.

The hot slice of his blade catches my face, and I hiss from the pain. Ashera's gasping for air, and I am torn between caring for her and killing this motherfucker. With my other hand, I grasp his wrist and slam his hand onto the ground beneath us. The blade falls away, but he isn't giving up that easily.

He pushes against me, our bodies raise into the air, hovering as I increase my hold on his wrist and throat. I feel the cold, rough skin of his fingers as one hand closes over the wrist of the hand at his throat. His other fist makes contact with my jaw as I fly across the room, slamming his body into the far wall. A painting explodes and pieces of the frame scatter, one of them impaling into his back. The scent of his freshly spilled blood urges me on.

Behind me, I hear grunts and hisses from the men who've come to protect their leader. Kieran grabs for my throat, but I dodge him, reaching for the six-inch piece of wood impaled in my shoulder. With speed and precision, I slam it into the side of his neck and grit my teeth as he shrieks. The more I twist the thick mass, the more blood spills.

Our bodies fall to the ground, and the air rushes out of my lungs when he strikes me in the sternum. I will not let him best me. My need for his death is too strong.

"Die, motherfucker," I snarl and dig my claws into the other side of his neck, feeling the flesh and muscle tear. Hot liquid pours over my hand, and his eyes go vacant from the blood loss. I know I have him. He's knocking on Lucifer's door.

We roll twice, stopping when I straddle his waist. With every ounce of energy in my body, I push my fingers into the open wound on the side of his neck, wrapping them around his vertebra. His eyes bulge as I tighten my grip. Kieran's body goes lax as a loud popping sound signals I've paralyzed him. If I don't kill him now, he will heal.

"This is for hurting what's mine," I rage, tearing his head from his body. A roar wrenches from my throat as I toss his head to the side.

I despise the demon that lives inside me for wanting more blood. The incubus part wants to destroy every living thing that poses a threat to him and the succubus that owns what's left of his human heart. She is his, and no one will ever take her from him again. My thirst for vengeance will never be tamed when it comes to Ashera.

"Cassius!" Victor bellows. When I shake the bloodlust from my mind, I glance around the room and see the bodies of Kieran's men. They're in pieces as my gargoyles and the ones who came to help are nursing their own wounds.

The demon disappears as soon as I see Victor on his knees, his wrist pressing against Ashera's lips. There isn't anything for me to clean my hands with as I cross the room. I don't want to touch her with that demon's blood on me.

I don't know if I said it aloud or if Xavier already knew, but he thrusts his shirt into my hands as

I cross the room. I clean myself as best as I can before falling to my knees.

"My love," I whisper as I lean over her face. Her eyes aren't as dead as they were while she was on her knees next to Kieran's desk. The fucking collar and leash are still around her neck, and it's covered in her blood. Someone has already removed the silver shackle, and her eyes are filling with blood.

I can't see her collared like that. It's too much. My hands move frantically over the clasp, ripping it away from her skin as soon as it comes free. As soon as it is gone, she blinks, and I see life rush back into her gaze, but her face is starting to pale from the loss of blood.

"Cass," she breathes. "You came."

"I'll always come for you, Ashera," I promise and scoop her up off the floor. She turns her face into my neck as I disappear from the house. I don't know what Victor will do, but I hope he torches the place.

Salvatore is waiting for us the moment I reappear in the foyer of our home. His eyes flash red. "Everything is prepared in your room."

I nod and take her up the stairs. Fagan has drawn a bath and left several towels on the floor for cleanup. I use my own magic to remove my clothes and step into the water. Ashera sighs as we sink below the warmth.

"I'm okay," she vows, touching my cheek. "I just shut down while he had me again."

"You're also weak," I say, using my thumb to touch underneath her eye. She needs energy and more blood. I'm not too far behind her on the depletion.

"We both are," she agrees and scoops water up in her hand, using it to clean dried blood off my arm. "Let's bathe. Then we will feed."

"First, I want to know what happened," I inquire, reaching for a cloth and soap. She doesn't immediately talk, and I don't push her. Instead, I clean her upper body, focusing on the blood where her throat was slit. The wound has healed, thanks to Victor's blood.

"He tried to have sex with me, but I fought him," she admits. I feel my anger bubbling beneath the surface, but I hold it back. She's been through another abduction, and I'm sure she won't react well to seeing my demon for who he really is.

It's easy to remember she's new to this life. In some ways, she's naïve to our ways, but in others, she fits right in. We're products of Lucifer. We have to have human blood and souls to live. There isn't ever going to be a time we can live off of each other.

"You did well." I praise her while I continue to wash away the blood from both of our bodies. The water is starting to turn a pink color, and I should probably drain the tub, but she's curled up against me. I don't want to let her go just yet.

"Are the gargoyles available for feedings?" she asks, tilting her head back so she can look into my eyes. She touches my jaw with her soft fingers, and I close my eyes when she presses her lips to mine. "I need to feed, but I want to make love to you first. I need this, Cassius."

"I need you, too," I whisper and kiss her softly for several seconds.

I toe the drain and carefully stand from the tub. Ashera wraps her legs around my waist as I walk us toward the bed. Her lips are soft, but her kisses are demanding. I can scent her, and my cock hardens as she rubs her pussy up and down my shaft while I attempt to get us to the bed.

She doesn't stop kissing me as I lay her down, finding her core with ease. I don't know how long we can handle making love to each other in our conditions, but I'm going to try to stay with her for as long as I can.

"Call down and have the gargoyles come up in ten minutes," she begs, rolling her hips up so I sink deeper into her body. "We're going to need them."

Chapter 17
Ashera

I feel my powers draining faster than he can give me energy. We're both weak, and as bad as I would prefer to spend the night with him buried between my legs, we need blood and sex from someone else.

A knock on the door signals the gargoyles who were brought here for us. Briley and Lacey enter with Laran, and they don't hesitate to undress. My fangs extend as I eye Briley's vein. It throbs as her steel-gray eyes darken.

Gargoyles are our servants in so many ways. Cassius told me we could feed off of them in a pinch, but usually they don't like to because it takes the gargoyles away from their usual tasks of caring for the Incubi's home.

"Ms. Andrews," Briley greets me, laying down next to me. Cassius slips from my body and I feel the loss, but I don't protest. Briley takes my nipple between her middle and forefinger, rolling it until I moan from the pinch of pain. "I'm here for your needs, mistress."

"As are we," Laran announces, taking Lacey's hand. They approach the bed, and I find the energy to reach up and pull Lacey down on my other side. The three of us are laying there with our legs hanging off the bed at our knees.

"Cassius, fuck her," I order, pointing to Lacey. She's beautiful with hair a shade darker than my own. Seeing him stalk her with his hand on his cock excites me.

"Laran, tend to my mate and her new play toy." Cassius nods toward Briley. "I saw you eyeing the vein in her neck, my love."

Briley's hair is short and jet black. There's enough for a handful when I tangle my fingers in it, making a fist to bring her to my lips. She tastes of power, and I feel Laran at my pussy. His cock is hot against my core as he nestles himself between my legs.

The room is dark, but I do not need light to see as I release the female gargoyle. Lacey moans beside me as Cassius takes her pussy and wraps his hands around her thick hips, slowing thrusting into her body. His eyes haven't left mine, and I know he's making silent promises of things to come after we feed.

"Laran," I moan and reach for his cock, guiding it into my body. His body is made for pleasure, and I pant as he buries himself at my core. His energy bleeds into me immediately, and I feel the need overcome me. My head swivels, and I need blood. Briley sees the need in my eyes and comes in, turning her neck to face me at the last second.

I strike her vein with no warning, blood filling my mouth. I drink and roll my hips, silently telling

Laran I need him just as much. I'm beyond weak from my encounter with Kieran. I will never tell Cassius that my maker fed off of me for the first four hours I was in his dungeon again. There are things I will keep to myself, and I will hold it for eternity.

"Mistress?" Briley calls out. Her voice is fading.

I hiss at Cassius as he pulls her away. My demon wants to protect its prey, and I realize I'm in need of more blood than I thought. Laran's eyes widen when I come off the bed, wrapping my legs around his waist in one swift movement. His cock never leaves my body as I strike his vein. The male turns and sits on the bed, holding me tight. I feel his cock swell, and I know I'm about to receive the blast of energy I need.

When my eyes scan the room, I see Cassius at Lacey's neck, his hips thrusting as he finds his own release. His eyes are cast upward so they're tracking my every move. I hear him growl as he's taking what he needs to refuel. Briley is sitting up on the bed, already recovered from my attack. Her steel-gray eyes darken as she licks her lips. She's aching for release, and I want to give that to her.

My body jerks as Laran comes, his energy like a strike of lightning to my system. I feel my power explode, and the demon inside me snarls, pushing away from the male to stand. He falls back on the bed, panting from his release.

Briley moves to face me as I stalk her. Cassius releases his hold on Lacey's hip to stroke my hair as I crawl toward the other gargoyle. My eyes are only on her. "Lay down, gargoyle. I want to taste you."

The female sighs and lays on her back as I slide my hands between her legs. She's wet for me, and I take my time giving her what she's craving while I take what I need from her.

Chapter 18
Cassius

My mate is giving the gargoyle the wildest orgasm, and my cock swells again inside Lacey from the sight before me. I've fed, and I want more, but the female beneath me is spent. I cannot take anymore from her. Even in my state, I know it's too dangerous.

Laran has moved across the room to dress. He sits heavily in the chair by the door and leans over, resting his elbows on his knees. Briley has her hands buried in Ashera's hair, riding my mate's face with her impending release.

"I'm going to fuck your mouth, Briley," I announced as I climb on the bed.

"Please, master," she moans and reaches for me, tilting her head back to take me into her mouth.

The gargoyle shifts her hips rapidly as she swallows my cock. Ashera raises her eyes to look at me over Briley's mound. I see the corner of my mate's lips lift in a saucy smirk. I know she's enjoying this female, and I will have to talk to her owner to see if I can negotiate Briley's employment. Ashera will need a female to tend to her at the house, and I think this gargoyle is exactly what she needs.

"Make her come, Ashera," I order, leaning over to touch my mate's hair. The silky strands beneath my fingers urges me on to pump my seed into Briley's mouth. The moment I orgasm, she comes on my mate's tongue. The blast of energy from the gargoyle soaks into my soul, and I pull free of her mouth, falling back against the pillows. I watch as Ashera lifts from Briley's pussy to kiss the female as a way of saying thank you.

We all rest for several minutes. Naked bodies are sprawled out across my large bed. Laran is still in the chair across the room, and he's sitting up straight now. A gargoyle's energy will return quicker than a human's, and within twenty minutes, our guests have dressed and slipped out of the room.

"I want her," Ashera begs, a small pout tilting her bottom lip. I can't resist and lean over to nip at it.

"I'll speak with Caspian to see if we can hire her here to be your gargoyle," I promise and pull her body close to mine. "Now, I need to get some food."

"Can Fagan bring it in here? Because I have no desire to get dress or leave this room," she chuckles. As energized as we are, the marathon sex we had with the three gargoyles was tiring.

"Let me call down," I say, reaching for the phone.

Fagan brings a tray of food twenty minutes later, setting it on the top of the dresser by the door. He closes the door without a word, and I crawl from my spot to bring the tray over so we can eat in bed. By now, I've turned on the television and Ashera is watching a televised broadcast of a rock band she recently discovered and loves.

"I like their name," she admits as she bites into a piece of chicken. "I mean, Cycle of Sin *is* a badass name for a rock band."

"You have a point there," I reply. I'm not paying much attention to the television or the music playing. My eyes are only for her, and I can't believe she is mine.

"What's wrong?" she asks as she licks the spices off her fingertips.

"I didn't know I would find someone to make this life less miserable," I admit. She freezes mid-lick and drops her hand to her lap.

"Oh, Cassius," she coos and raises up on her knees, tackling me to the bed. The food spills on the floor, but I ignore it. The carpets can be cleaned. "I don't want you to think this life is miserable."

"It was until I found you," I explain.

"Me?" she laughs. "I'm not that interesting."

"You are everything," I whisper and capture her lips. My hand cups her face and I absorb her scent.

"Can we find love as demons?" she asks as I release her.

"I think we are still part human," I reply, kissing her quickly. "If there is such a thing as love among us, I'm very certain I found it with you."

"I love you, Cassius," she says, smiling as I cup her face again. "I still feel human in a lot of ways, and this is one thing Kieran couldn't take from me…my ability to love. He tried, but he didn't succeed."

"I will love you for an eternity, Ashera Andrews," I promise and roll her over. "I'm going to make love to you tonight."

"Take your time, Incubus."

Chapter 19
Ashera

I stand at the window and wait. It's been a month since I was saved from my maker. Cassius and I have found a new life together, living at Salvatore's mansion. He is my territory leader now, and he prefers we stay close.

Fagan hurries up the stairs behind me to finish preparations on the guest room that will now belong to my own personal gargoyle. Caspian agreed to us hiring Briley, and she is due to arrive any moment.

Cassius flew her first class from Washington. I've planned a shopping trip for her as soon as she gets settled. I want her comfortable here. My mate told me I didn't have to spoil her, but I ignored him. I want her to be happy.

"Here she comes!" I yell for the entire household to hear.

Cassius, Sal, and Vic exit from the office while Memphis, Xavier, and Fagan all descend the stairs. I wrench the door open and meet the cab driver.

"You're here!" I giggle and pull her into my arms. We hug while Cassius and Fagan remove her bags from the trunk. "Come inside. We have your room ready."

"Thank you for hiring me," she blushes. "I'm so happy to be here."

"Come on," I urge, pulling her by the hand. As

soon as we walk inside, the males leave us and we hurry up the stairs. Her room is next to ours, and I push the door open wide. "We will go shopping after you've rested and get you whatever you need."

"Thank you, but I'm here to serve *you*," she reminds me.

"Right now, I want you to get comfortable," I urge and pull her over to a chair by the window. "Fagan has a meal schedule, and he sticks to it. You do not have to come to dinner if you'd like to sleep. I know you've had a long day getting here."

"I want to work," Briley states, looking around the room. "It's in my nature to do for my mistress."

"I know," I laugh, shaking my head. "I really wish you'd just call me Ashera."

"Oh, I…um, I guess I can," she stammers. "Is there anything you need from me? Do you need to feed?" She asks the question, but I see a heat in her eyes.

"Maybe later," I answer honestly. Fagan arrives with her bags, setting them inside the walk-in closet. Her room is almost identical to my own, and she has her own bathroom. "I'll leave you to get situated."

"Thank you," she says and I leave her to unpack.

Cassius is at the kitchen table, pouring a glass of wine. He holds up an empty glass. "Drink?"

"Please," I reply and take a seat next to his.

"You know, we should talk about what

happened at Kieran's," he begins, but like I've done over the last few days, I shake my head and deny his questions.

"I really don't want to talk about him," I say through gritted teeth.

"It's time we discuss his claim that you are able to bear children," he states, ignoring my denial.

"I think he is lying," I reply and sip my wine. Whatever that psycho motherfucker had to say is a lie in my eyes. He was a manipulator, a narcissist, and worse than anything the devil could produce. I hope he's rotting at the lowest pits of *Hades* right now.

"But what if he's not?" Cassius asks.

"I have yet to have a cycle," I tick off. "I've never had any type of fertile days where I felt like a dog in heat, and I sure as hell don't have any cravings to be a mother."

"We've been doing research," he informs me, taking a healthy sip of his drink. The faraway look in his eyes worries me. It wasn't until recently that he admitted he hated the fact he was still alive after all this time. If it wasn't for me, he would've roamed this earth a miserable man until the end of time.

"What type of research?" I press, needing to know what he knows.

"There are others like you," he reveals. "There are succubi who've reared children."

"We don't know if I am one of those women," I remind him. "Kieran was a sadist, and he wanted power. There's no way he could've known I was one of those women. All he did was fuck me, feed from me, slit my throat, and bury me in the ground until I had to claw my way out."

I don't mention the torturing part. Cassius has no business knowing those details. Kieran is dead, and bringing up what happened wouldn't do anything other than cause my mate grief…grief he didn't need to experience.

"I would like for you to see a doc…" he begins, but I stand up quickly from my seat.

"No, Cassius!" I walk over to the sink and set my empty glass inside. "And that's final."

I don't want to see any doctors. I'm fucking immortal, and I *died* that day almost a year ago. There is no fucking way I can get pregnant.

None.

Not happening…

Ever.

The End…

Look for more from Cassius and Ashera
Coming Soon…

A Letter from the Author:

Hello loves!

I hope you enjoyed Thirst. It was so much fun to write, and I hope you enjoyed meeting Cassius and Ashera.

This book was on fire from the moment I opened the computer to write the beginning of their story. Once I had the idea, the words flowed, and I was able to write it in just under 11 days. I've never written a book that quickly before, and I can't wait to dive into book 2 in this trilogy.

Cassius and Ashera have quite a challenge on their hands, being as they cannot live off of each other's blood and energy. The story surrounding the gargoyles intrigues me. I want to know more about them, and I hope with the following books, they talk to me enough that I can someday write their story, too.

Be on the lookout for book 2 in the Incubus Tamed series later this spring/summer. The title will be called "Crave". It'll explore more into their relationship and the struggles they will have to overcome to be together as a mated pair.

If you loved it, leave a review, and if you aren't already following me on Bookbub, please take a moment to do so at the link below.

https://www.bookbub.com/authors/theresa-hissong

Thank you for reading!
Theresa Hissong

About Theresa Hissong:

Theresa Hissong is the bestselling author of the Rise of the Pride series. She writes paranormal romance, rockstar romance, and romantic suspense.

She enjoys spending her days and nights creating the perfect love affair, and she takes those ideas to paper. When she's not writing, Theresa spends her free time traveling and attending concerts all over the United States.

Look for other exciting reads…coming very soon!

57272613R00102

Made in the USA
Middletown, DE
29 July 2019